D0646047

# THE WINTER GARDEN

# THE WINTER GARDEN

*a novel by*

# JOHANNA VERWEERD

BETHANYHOUSE
Minneapolis, Minnesota

*The Winter Garden*
by Johanna Verweerd

Translated into English by HELEN RICHARDSON-HEWITT
Dutch edition, © 1995, *De sintertuin*, Uitgeverij Boekencentrum.
English edition, © 1996, Uitgeverij Boekencentrum.

Uitgeverij Boekencentrum,
PO Box 29, 2700 AA Zoetermeer
Netherlands
Tel. (0031) 79 3615481
Fax. (0031) 79 361489
Email boekencentrum@wxs.nl

Cover design by Uttley/DouPonce Designworks

All rights reserved. No part of this publication may be reproduced, stored in a
retrieval system, or transmitted in any form or by any means—electronic,
mechanical, photocopying, recording, or otherwise—without the prior written
permission of the publisher and copyright owners.

Published by Bethany House Publishers
A Ministry of Bethany Fellowship International
11400 Hampshire Avenue South
Bloomington, Minnesota 55438
www.bethanyhouse.com

Printed in the United States of America by
Bethany Press International, Bloomington, Minnesota 55438

**Library of Congress Cataloging-in-Publication Data**

Verweerd, Joke.
   [Wintertuin. English]
   The winter garden / Johanna Verweerd.
      p.  cm.
   ISBN 0-7642-2523-5
   I. Title.
   PT5881.32.E79 W5613      2001
   839.3'1364—dc21

00-012967

JOHANNA VERWEERD has gained a large audience among many different kinds of readers. Besides novels, she has written short stories, poetry, and film scripts. Verweerd frequently gives lectures on her work as a writer and is the president of the largest Christian authors association in the Netherlands. *The Winter Garden* is her first novel, published in Dutch, German, and now English. Since its first publication in 1995, Verweerd has written two other novels: *De rugzak* (*The Rucksack,* 1997) and *Permissie* (*Permission,* 1999). Her books have been reprinted several times. Johanna Verweerd and her husband live in Woubrugge near The Hague. They have a son and a daughter.

## CHAPTER ONE

THE WEATHER FORECAST confirmed her foreboding—calm before the storm. This calm was a few exceptionally fine autumn days, too good really for the end of October. The damp fallen leaves lay stewing in the sun. All during the summer the sky had never been so steely blue. The people basked sleepily in the warmth, but Ika had a feeling of restlessness. The scent of the large bunch of chrysanthemums was nearly too strong for her.

Sea gulls circled high in the sky, another sign of a storm coming.

The storm broke after the letter. The letter had been waiting for Ika in her mailbox, and she stood with it now in her hand in the hallway of the block of flats. She automatically greeted the man from the flat below but didn't respond to his joke as he expected. In amazement he stood staring at her till the elevator doors closed. Ika took the stairs, which put off the moment. Meanwhile, she turned the letter over and over in her hand. It was her sister's handwriting. Of this there was no doubt. After all the years it was still the same—sensitive, childish copperplate handwriting.

*To Miss I. Boerema,* it read, with a curly *I* and a curly *B.* Who on Earth ever wrote *To Miss* anymore? This irritated Ika, though the formality was easier to cope with than the shock of getting the letter.

She was upstairs now and sitting on the sofa in the orange light that filtered into the room through the sunshade. She opened the letter and started to read.

The very first words brought a lump to her throat. *My dear Ika.* They hadn't spoken to or seen each other for fifteen years, but she still wrote *My dear Ika.* The picture of her sister as Ika remembered her loomed up at her between the lines. Nelly with her little, round kittenish face, her slightly crookedly spaced eyes and springy blond hair. Fifteen years! Slowly the contents of the letter sank in. Mother was ill, an incurable illness.

*You'll have to come soon, Ika, if that's what you want. According to Dr. Spaan, she won't last much longer. She's already on the waiting list for the nursing home as I'm not able to be with her all the time. I've got the boys to look after too. Dirk-Willem is still only six, and it would be too much for Mother if we moved in with her.*

What lay behind all these words? How long had Mother been ill? How much had Nelly had to put up with? Nelly, who had always been spared such hardship.

Ika glanced at the envelope in her lap. On the front was *Boerema,* and on the back, *sender: Peters-de Haan.* This said enough in itself, and yet she'd never in all these many years felt so close to

Nelly. Blood relatives, though you'd never have guessed it from the names on the envelope.

The sunlight drew stripes in front of her eyes, and the room shuddered in a mist of tears.

❦

Nelly was five years younger than Ika and the little ray of sunshine in the house.

"Now, look after her well, Ika! You're the oldest. When you're crossing the road, hold her hand tightly. And make sure you get her to Miss Toms's class." Mother's face looked anxious, as it often did when it came to Nelly.

Unaware of any problem, Nelly stretched her new dress along her legs. *It was such a lovely dress*, Ika thought, *nice enough to be a Sunday dress.* It was blue corduroy with little white stars and puffy sleeves. Nelly was a little princess. Her hair was curled in ringlets that danced whenever she jumped.

Ika was proud of her but also jealous. Her washed-out white blouse pulled out of her too short skirt at the back, and she never had enough bobby pins for her spiky hair. Nodding furiously, Ika promised to do everything that her mother demanded.

Ika felt she was a big girl, for although this was Nelly's first time going to school, she was in the sixth class now. "Come on, I'll bring you to Miss Toms, right into the classroom. The older boys can't pester you there."

"Why should they pester me?" asked Nelly's voice behind her.

"I don't know why. Just because they want to. Because they think you're stupid."

Nelly's face fell, and her eyes looked more uneven than usual.

Ika quickly said, "But not you, Nelly. Don't be scared. I'll be with you."

Then Ika pursed her lips firmly together. If those boys tried to bother Nelly on her first day, then she would stand up for her sister. If necessary Ika would let them hit her so that nothing happened to Nelly. Because if Father were to find out that Nelly had been mistreated . . . Ika shuddered at the thought.

"Nelly, can you run fast?" Ika suddenly asked. "Just run for a little while, but as fast as you can." When she was satisfied, Ika said, "You've got to run like that while I keep the mean boys away."

"What mean boys?"

Ika said nothing as she grasped Nelly's hand firmly in hers. *Just let them try!* she thought.

Ika felt strong and important now that Nelly was walking beside her. It gave her a new dignity. And Nelly was so pretty with her curls and her new dress. But when the torrent of swearing, pushing, and kicking broke out, Nelly didn't need to run her fastest. The boys left her undisturbed. Everything rained down on Ika's narrow back till she was dizzy and sick and had to vomit in a corner of the playground, a place where the teacher on duty never went.

*My dear Ika,* Nelly wrote, and the words made Ika feel better.

It grew suddenly dark in the room, so Ika got up and opened the blinds. She put the kettle on for tea, then dried the already dry plate from breakfast with the tea towel, and her wet eyes too. When the kettle began to whistle, she was still standing there, leaning against the kitchen counter.

Mother was ill, and Nelly thought she ought to know about it.

Ika walked over and closed the windows. The wind whistled through the cracks, and the balcony door slammed shut with a bang, its pane rattling.

She should write a letter back to Nelly and maybe also to Mother. Yet, after Ika had the blank writing pad in front of her, she couldn't find the words. She couldn't figure out how to begin. Fifteen years is a long time.

She looked around the room. Mother had never been here, nor had Nelly. All they knew about her flat was the address. Good thing she hadn't moved in the meantime.

The clouds grew darker, and then the first drops of rain began to fall. Ika reread the letter. It was exactly like the other times when mail had arrived from home—the announcement of Father's death and Nelly's wedding invitation—as if a blanket were smothering her, or as if she were being pulled down into a pit.

Nelly wrote about the boys. *Dirk-Willem is only six.* She hadn't realized it till then. Nelly was a mother, and Willem a father. Ika couldn't imagine this. Willem Peters, the pale boy, who on his sixteenth birthday had been given the most expensive motor scooter his parents could find. She'd often thought of Willem's parents as show-offs, always wanting to have more than other people.

This was Nelly's husband and the father of her nephews. She was an aunt! A smile began to play slowly around her mouth. Auntie Ika. *My dear Ika . . .*

What should she do? Not eat, that was clear. Her stomach was churning. Tea and more tea, that was the answer. Tea was at least warm and friendly, a pain-killer too. The pressure above her eyes didn't bode well.

While she pressed the tablet from its strip, Ika sighed deeply as she remembered the fear that had awakened her the night before. Sweating and with her heart thumping, she had shot upright in her bed. She couldn't recall the dream, only the threat of something terrible that had gripped her by the throat. She didn't dare try to sleep again, but had lain awake for hours, watching and waiting for dawn to come. Her premonitions hardly ever deceived her.

Just take two tablets and listen to the singing of the kettle and the roaring of the storm. Mother was incurably ill. *My dear Ika . . .*

In the middle of the night Ika sat up in bed again, shocked by a question that entered her throbbing head. *Did Mother ask for me? Did she ask if I would come? Does she really want to see me? Or did Nelly take the initiative?* There being no answers only led to more and more questions. Did it matter if Mother had asked for her? Did it make any difference if her going to see Mother had been Nelly's initiative?

The dark bedroom slowly took on the contours of the living room of her parents' house.

Ika looked around with the duster still in her hand. She was thirteen, and with Mother's apron on, she looked as if she was getting breasts. Had she not looked after everything for six weeks? All the time that Mother had been in the hospital, Ika had been the mother in the house. She had washed, cooked, ironed, and had even cleaned the outside of the house once a week. This is how Father had wanted it. Things mustn't get untidy while Mother was sick. And now that Mother was coming home, everything had to be extra neat. She had even picked the dead blossoms off the geraniums in the window box. Mother always did this too. And the apple pie in the oven smelled lovely. Everything was ready. Mother could come home.

All the cleaning had taken a long time, as Ika rushed back and forth across the house. Were the sheets in Mother's bedroom smoothed just right? Was there a handkerchief under the pillow beside the clean nightie?

She put water on for coffee. Mother liked things to be shiny. "If the kettle and the taps stay shiny, then the kitchen looks clean," she always said. Besides, the methylated alcohol smelled so clean and nice.

Ika looked at her face, which appeared chubby and distorted in the reflection off the kettle. What a large mouth she had. With a shriek, she threw the duster. It had burst into flames from the methylate.

At that moment Ika heard a car on the gravel. Father! And with Mother! In one fell swoop, she had picked up the burning cloth and, in a desperate gesture, clasped it to her chest. The burnt aroma shot sharply up her nostrils. Calm and clearheaded now, she turned on the tap and tossed the blackened cloth into the sink, a sizzling little heap. The smell was dreadful.

Then came Father's footsteps at the door.

Ika turned over. Don't think about Father! She had to get to sleep. Another busy day faced her tomorrow, and if the headache didn't go away, then she would be worth nothing. She put her hand to her eyes. It felt warm and heavy. She counted from one to a hundred. She thought about the sea, about waves of rest and regularity.

"Where's Nelly?" asked Mother. What a white face she had, and her eyes looked so strange. Her hair was lying loose all over the pillow. Thin, dark hair with gray stripes, but very long.

"At Carien's house," answered Ika immediately. "I was supposed to go and get her, but first everything else had to be ready."

"Do you call this ready?" Father yelled, glaring at her. "The whole place smelling of fire just when your mother gets home. Where's your common sense?"

"Never mind, Dirk," Mother said weakly. "She's already had her punishment. I'd like to see Nelly now."

So Ika ran outside to look for Nelly. It was only after Nelly had crashed down on her knees beside Mother's bed that Ika dared to examine her hands. Blisters. They would sting when she had to do the dishes.

Had Mother asked for her this time? Did she say, "Nelly, I'd love to see Ika once more. I'd really like Ika . . ."

Oh, Mother was incurably ill, and Nelly had written *My dear Ika* . . . Crying and headaches were a bad combination. She knew this from experience.

But what else could she do?

## CHAPTER TWO

"I CAN TELL, don't say anything. Just go and sit down and I'll get some coffee!"

These were the words that greeted Ika when she stepped into the little office beside the workshop.

Big and burly behind the desk, Simone Berger stood up, sending her chair scraping back across the linoleum. Ika clutched at her head.

"Sorry!" said the boss with a wry smile at Ika's contorted face.

Simone came back in with two mugs of coffee and sat down opposite Ika. After a pause, she picked up her chair as if it weighed nothing and moved it closer to Ika.

"So what's up?"

Ika looked at the rough face of her boss. The features all seemed too coarse, and yet it was an attractive face. Forceful, but in a friendly way, with the warmest brown eyes and flawless though irregular teeth. The cropped, dark blond hair gave her a masculine appearance, as did her walk and loud voice. Simone Berger, the owner of Berger's Landscape Gardening, was admired and envied for her drive and success. She was a first-rate businesswoman, though only a few people knew how honest yet efficient she was in her work.

For Ika, Simone was invaluable.

"I have a bad headache."

"Yes, I can see that. But even so, do you have to look like that?"

Ika warmed her hands on the mug, hesitating whether to say anything or not. Simone shifted her position, leaning backward till her chair creaked, and then interlaced her hands behind her neck and waited.

Ika stifled a smile. A bulky woman like Simone shouldn't sit like that, not that way, with her enormous bosom off balance with the chair's legs. The dark blue sweater looked too small, though the label XXL was as usual showing at Simone's neck. *It's odd how some people can't keep that sort of thing tucked in*, thought Ika. The loops on Simone's pants, and on her skirts on the rare occasions she wore them, always slipped out of view.

Simone kept on looking as only she could look. Not angrily. Not kindly. Not threateningly. *But stubbornly.* She would sit there until Ika said something.

Ika sighed, realizing she'd have to jump in at the deep end. If she told about the letter, the letter and Nelly's question would take possession of her. She would inevitably have to protect Nelly and Mother from Simone's scrutiny. She would start defending them, explaining things away, thinking up excuses, and she didn't know whether she wanted to do that or not. If she were to talk to Simone, she'd have to take sides. It was unavoidable.

Mr. Molenaar, the teacher, had brown eyes that saw everything, especially the things his pupils didn't want him to see. Ika felt this immediately when she walked into his class, the fifth class. Mr. Molenaar liked the fifth class, he always said, because the children aren't real big yet, but they're a long way from being little.

In Mr. Molenaar's class, the students got their own tables and chairs rather than having to share a desk. Though the tables were placed neatly two in a row, it still gave Ika the feeling of having her own spot, allowing her to fidget if she wanted to. A sort of independence went with the fifth class. And with Mr. Molenaar. After all, he always said that children had to grow into people. Ika often had to think about that. It seemed so logical. First a person's a child, and then later that person becomes a grown-up. But the way the teacher explained this, it had more meaning, like a task or something.

A headache—that had earlier been called a stomachache—forced Ika to lay her head on her arms.

The teacher could see clearly that something was wrong. "Go on home, Ika."

She shook her head. Not home. Father wouldn't like that. He would think Ika was slacking if she gave up and went home early.

He would tell her, "If I stopped work every time something was wrong, you wouldn't even have stale bread to eat!"

The teacher's eyes softened. "Then take a little nap at your desk, with your head resting on your arms like that. We'll try to work quietly."

It was warm. The table steamed up with her breath. It smelled of varnish and school. She didn't want to cry. Why did she always feel like crying when somebody was nice to her? Or when somebody looked at her like the teacher had just done—so kindly.

The bell made Ika jump. Had she really been asleep all this time? The arithmetic exercise books had already been collected. She sat up straight, feeling embarrassed as she looked down. Using her sleeve, she quickly wiped up the small pool of spittle on the table.

The teacher gave thanks. The usual daily prayer, but always said a shade different each time. Ika flushed when the teacher asked God to give them all a good night's rest and strength for tomorrow, to come back to their work well-rested and alert. He had asked this for her.

When the classroom began to empty, the teacher approached her. "Ika, have you told your parents how often you get these stomachaches?"

Ika shook her head, but then nodded. The teacher smiled and raised her face with his hand under her chin.

"You've got the creases from your sleeve on your forehead," he said. Then when the classroom went quiet, which made Ika even more embarrassed, he asked, "Are you still being teased much?" His eyes looked as if he hoped she'd say no.

So she said it. "No. Oh no, sir, not every day. I always run out of school very fast and go through Juliana Street. They don't know that."

"But isn't that the wrong way?"

"Yes, exactly."

A mischievous though pained expression crossed the teacher's eyes. "You're a clever girl, Ika. Is everything all right at home . . . with your mother, I mean?"

Ika nodded enthusiastically. "Dr. Spaan says she's completely better again. But I still keep on helping her a lot. For you never know . . . and Father says that Satan finds some mischief still for idle hands to do."

The teacher laughed. It was great to be able to talk to the teacher like this—straightforwardly, like adults.

"Does your sister help as well?"

"No, Nelly's far too small."

"Off you go now," he said. "And you don't need to go home on Juliana Street. The boys have long since gone."

Simone was still looking at her. She just sighed now and then.

"Okay, you do know how to keep up the pressure," Ika said.

"Well," Simone said, sliding back into her normal position

again, her arms on the desk, "get it off your chest then."

"My mother's very ill."

Simone's eyebrows shot up, and her head inclined forward. "Who?"

"My mother," Ika repeated. "I got a letter from my sister, Nelly, yesterday." The eyebrows again. "Come on, Simone . . ." Ika raised her hands in apology.

Simone leaned in toward Ika. "So what's wrong with her?"

"I don't really know. In the letter Nelly writes 'incurably,' and that the doctor says she won't live much longer. She's apparently on a list to be admitted to a nursing home, because Nelly can't look after her around the clock like Mother needs. Nelly has a family of her own now."

"Is that so?"

The hint of a smile crept over Ika's face. In all she said and did, Simone showed her loyalty to her friend.

"In the letter she talks about 'the boys,' who I presume are her sons."

"Do you know if your mother asked Nelly to write this letter?"

The hurt expression around Ika's mouth and the slight shrug of her shoulders answered Simone's question.

Simone stood up and bent over the desk, getting so close to Ika that she could smell Simone's breath. "I don't think much of these people, Ika! For fifteen years you've been like an outcast, the black sheep of the family. What am I saying? Not fifteen years, more like your whole life! But now that your sister needs your help with your mother, she all of a sudden thinks you're good enough. Can't you see you're being used?"

Ika laid a tired hand over her eyes. What could she say to show Simone the confusing thoughts and feelings she was struggling with inside? "I can't think about the motives of Mother or Nelly right now, but only my own. I've got to try to see a way out of what I'm feeling. All these years haven't I in some way or another had a frustrated longing for home? Haven't I been crippled by feelings of guilt?"

Oh, those eyes of Simone's. She always had to look at Ika like that, carrying on as if she'd won the Nobel Prize for defending human rights.

"For sure the answer to your last question is *yes*," Simone said.

Simone made three steps and then took a swing at the filing cabinet, because the lowest drawer always needed a good kick to make it spring open. She must have hit it hard, for she limped a bit afterward.

The green-painted shed stood at the back of the garden. Like the house, the shed had red and white shutters. Ika loved the shed. She often played "House" there. She made a little table and a seat out of some boxes. Annelies, the doll, rested in a cardboard box with a cover made out of the old curtain from the front room. Ika glanced around. What else could she do to make it look more real?

If only she could use Nelly's tea set. And lemonade and biscuits from Mother. Where had Nelly gone? If Nelly played with her, then she'd be allowed the tea set. And if Nelly asked Mother for lemonade and biscuits . . . Yes, Ika would promise to tidy everything up again so that Father would never notice that they'd been playing in the shed.

Ika went to look for Nelly. When she saw the tea set in Nelly's bedroom, she wondered whether she should go ahead and take it with her. But no, she didn't dare touch it. Mother didn't like them to take each other's things without asking first. What would happen if Nelly started a quarrel?

After Ika returned, she found Nelly by the shed. She told her the plan, and Nelly agreed. "Only if I can be the mother!" Nelly said.

Ika bit her lip. She hated having to play the father. "Can I be your friend then, who lives with you?" But Nelly had misgivings, because there had to be a father. So Ika added, "I'll be your very best friend who has come from a faraway country! And we don't have a father . . . because he's dead."

Nelly nodded, then went to ask Mother for the lemonade, while Ika fetched the tea set. Stuffing it into her skirt, Ika attempted to carry it all at once.

Mother scolded her for this. "Whoever runs around like that, in their panties with their skirt up! If your father saw that . . ."

Nelly was already back in the shed with the lemonade, when

Ika stepped in and began placing the tea set pieces on the table. She was still standing by the door, when Ika rushed out again to ask Mother if she could borrow the mat in front of the door for a little while. In Ika's haste she had pulled the shed door closed. Two steps further on she heard Nelly's screams, high-pitched and full of pain. She knew before she looked. The shed door! Nelly's fingers were trapped! Nelly had turned white from the shock. Ika hurried her screaming little sister inside the house.

"Quick, Nelly, under the tap! Then you won't feel it as much!"

Mother wasn't in the kitchen. Thank goodness Mother wasn't there! Maybe she could calm Nelly down before Mother came in.

"Please try to quiet down, Nelly! And keep holding your fingers under the cold water. You can *always* be the mother, do you hear? Always! And I'll be the father from now on, okay?"

The crying grew somewhat less and changed to a subdued sobbing. Ika examined the injured little hand. The nails weren't blue, but on two of them there was a deep pinch mark that stood out white against the edge, growing ever redder.

When Mother walked in, Nelly began to cry loudly again. Mother pushed Ika away and held Nelly's hand under the tap herself. Ika stammered that it all had been an accident.

But Mother's eyes were angry, cold looking. She turned and shouted, "You! Get outside right now!"

Ika was already on her way. With tears in her eyes, she stood in the shed's doorway and stared at her makeshift house. From a distance she could still hear Nelly crying and her mother's soothing voice. It was all Ika's fault.

She placed her fingers on the doorjamb, closed her eyes, and banged the door shut: The pain burned up to her shoulder and stayed like a sharp dagger in the pit of her stomach. She looked at her throbbing fingers where the pain was concentrated. Her entire hand trembled. One nail was split open and the blood was dripping onto the tiles. But the other nail—the one that had turned purple—hurt the most. The pain was unbearable yet somehow felt good. It was her fault, so she had to feel it.

Simone looked up from her work. Ika had just put down the phone after making a business call. "Shouldn't you ring the doctor first?" Simone asked.

"Dr. Spaan?"

"Yes, your mother's family doctor. It seems sensible to me to find out exactly what's wrong with your mother. Look, 'incurable' can last for years. Your mother has always been weak and sickly. Those kind of people can hold on for a long time, Ika."

"It was more a way of life for Mother. If she was ill, then she got more attention, was able to get out of things and call on us. As soon as she was better, Father would begin kicking up a fuss again. Really the times when Mother was sick were a relief for us. Then at least he kept quiet." Even while she was saying this, Ika was shocked by the word *us*. By it she meant herself and Nelly. But had they ever been *us*?

Simone appeared perplexed. "Why did that man ever marry your mother, anyway?"

"I don't know. There are many things I don't know. We were never allowed to speak about the past. About who my father really was or how I came about. Was it rape? Or did my mother have a boyfriend at the time? The only thing that I know is that, thanks to me, life was made impossible. My coming into the world was a scandal. You couldn't imagine it, Simone, but a man like my grandfather, my mother's father, was no ordinary person. A minister in the church had at that time a lot of influence and maybe still has. He was so looked up to. And then suddenly to have a daughter who was pregnant. It wasn't for nothing that my mother kept quiet about it till the end. Maybe Grandfather arranged her marriage later on. I can imagine that of him. He would've been thankful to get a farmer's son to marry his sullied daughter."

Simone sighed. "I never could understand such straight-laced people. I don't know much about Christianity, but to my mind they give the wrong impression of it. Shouldn't your grandfather have set a better example of Christian forgiveness and love when his daughter was caught like that?"

"Stop talking about it, Simone! Do you really think I should phone the doctor?"

"Ika, sometimes I could shake you!" The telephone directory

landed on Ika's desk with a thud. With her hand already on the doorknob, Simone turned around and said, "I'm off now, first to Vertoren's, and then to see the architect of the Promenade Hotel to check up on the measurements. Then this afternoon you and I can draw up an estimate for the project. When I come back, your headache will have eased and you will have spoken to that doctor!"

Ika looked up with a start. "But shouldn't I negotiate with Vertoren?"

"No! Not with the headache you got. That smooth talker will take you for a ride. Did you hear me?"

"Yes, boss. You know, you should've been a sergeant in the military."

The brown eyes lit up just a little, though the voice remained under control. "And that's what I am too—for you anyway. It's people like you who people like me have to protect." The sound of the door slamming made Ika reach for her head for the umpteenth time.

She had seen Dr. Spaan more often at their home than at the clinic. He always came to the house for Mother, often shaking his head when he first saw her. Ika could only remember one time when she'd been with Mother at the clinic. That time it had been about her. The school's doctor had been very insistent that Mother take Ika's stomachaches more seriously. "Oh, she's always having a stomachache," Mother had said, "but it always clears up by itself."

The school's doctor had looked sternly over his half-rimmed glasses. From Mother to Ika and then back again. They were funny, those glasses. Ika had never seen anything like them.

"Ma'am, children who have frequent stomachaches run the risk of suffering from migraines later on. You see, children localize pain in their stomachs."

Mother had shrugged her shoulders, something she always did if she didn't understand. To add to this, the doctor had used pretty difficult words. Give her Dr. Spaan any day. He at least spoke plain English.

The indignation could be heard in her voice as Mother started to speak in Dr. Spaan's clinic. As if she had nothing better to do but to listen to the nonsense dished up by a school doctor. Dr. Spaan looked at the card in front of him. There wasn't much on it. Only Ika's name and address and a note about an infection in the middle ear.

"She's never sick, Doctor. You know that yourself. In that much she's lucky—she hasn't got my disposition."

Dr. Spaan gave her a slight nod, then suddenly and unexpectedly asked, "Why on earth did you give your child such an awful name?"

The blood drained from Mother's cheeks. "That has nothing to do with you and is none of your business! If I were you, I'd limit my inquiries to the practice of medicine!" she shouted.

She stood up, smoothed down her skirt, and pulled Ika by the arm toward the exit. Dr. Spaan said nothing, only looked at her blankly. Later that evening, Mother had said to Father that maybe they better start going to the new doctor. Dr. Spaan wasn't what he used to be.

But Father wouldn't hear of it. A person knew where he stood with Dr. Spaan, he had said. Besides, modernists like that new doctor weren't their sort of people.

No one talked about Ika's stomachaches again.

She found the telephone number right away.

"Dr. Spaan's receptionist speaking."

"Hello, this is Ika Boerema. I would like to speak to Dr. Spaan, please."

"What is it about?"

Ika sighed. "I'd prefer to tell him that myself."

"What was your name again?"

Ika spelled out her name, and while the receptionist repeated her name slowly, syllable by syllable, she heard in the background the bass voice of Dr. Spaan. Ika could understand word for word what he was saying.

"Put her on my extension," he said.

## CHAPTER THREE

"THERE'S NO GETTING away from it," he had said. "Your mother has tried everything, but there's no cure. The lung cancer is in an advanced stage and has spread to her brain. The only thing I can do is to see that she doesn't have much pain."

"How long do you think?" Ika asked.

"Three months at the most. Might well be shorter than that."

She thanked him and was about to hang up when she heard he was still saying something and so asked him if he'd repeat his question.

"Are you coming to see her soon?"

What was she to say? What did he know?

"It was to depend on this telephone call," she said honestly.

"Well?"

There was a long silence.

"I don't know."

"There are some decisions that you can put off, but not this one, Ikabod Boerema!"

His calling her by her full name made her throw down the receiver at once.

It had been her birthday that day, that Sunday. Ten years old and she felt really big now. She'd received new shoes on Saturday, for her birthday, and because she needed them. Father believed in useful presents. From Granddad she'd received a bag to take to church. It was a blue shoulder bag, which fastened with a shiny clasp. She got the bag on Saturday, too, because they never celebrated birthdays on Sundays. On Sunday they went to church, then to Sunday school, then back to church again later on. Father and Ika, anyhow. Mother always stayed at home with Nelly in the evenings.

Ika was looking forward to Sunday school, for then she could show off her new handbag and shoes. Not that she'd do this openly. Ika would simply walk in a way where all the children would notice her new things, especially the girls at school who had laughed at her worn-out shoes. She went to sit at the corner of the row of chairs.

The Sunday-school teacher turned out to be Mr. Van der Hoek, one of the church elders. Which was a pity. Ika had hoped it would be Miss Toms, who always told the stories so much better, even if sometimes it became a bit childish. Mr. Van der Hoek began by reading a long passage from the Bible. Then came the singing time, which was followed by everyone reciting the verses they had memorized during the previous week. Afterward, there wasn't much time left for the story.

During the reading, Ika sat repeating her text over and over again to herself. It was a hard one this time.

*"Remember ye not the former things, neither consider the things of old. Behold, I will do a new thing. Now it shall spring forth. Shall ye not know it? I will even make a way in the wilderness and streams in the desert."*

She recited the words in her head five times. She wanted to get the full four points on her birthday. This was the highest mark she could get.

Suddenly Ika noticed it was quiet and that all the children were looking at her. Why? Did they know about her new shoes? Or was it something else? Her cheeks flushed fiery red. Even the elder, Mr. Van der Hoek, was looking at her, and he had stopped his reading. Had he said her name or asked her a question and she hadn't heard? She looked around her, baffled. What was it, then?

Mr. Van der Hoek coughed and bent over his Bible again. "Because the ark of God was taken, and because of her father-in-law and her husband. And she said, 'The glory is departed from Israel, for the ark of God is taken.'"

Ika felt the blood draining from her head. She leaned against the back of the chair, feeling dizzy. Why were they all staring at her? What had the reading to do with her? She grew uneasy and scared. The text wouldn't work at all. She seemed instantly to have forgotten everything she had to say. The helper, one of the bigger girls, had to prompt her four times. Disappointed and confused,

Ika looked down at her card. Only one point. She'd be punished for that when she got home.

Mr. Van der Hoek began awkwardly, stammering as he proceeded to tell the story of Eli's death. Ika couldn't listen. Her head was full of an anxiety she struggled to understand. She pressed her new handbag against her stomach and then she didn't feel it so badly.

Only the last sentence in the story sank in, which had to do with Mr. Van der Hoek looking at her so fixedly.

"It was a shame for the people of Israel, a great shame. God is not mocked, boys and girls! The honor had been stolen, and the ark of God was in the hands of the heathen Philistines. That was why the dying mother named the child *Ichabod*. Shame. Let this be a lesson for us, that we can't go on living our lives as we were born—in sin. We must all appear before the judgment seat of God. And what will the verdict be?"

Nobody said a word to her when she ran off down the stone steps.

Yet the way they had looked at her was even worse than any scolding. When she got home she tried to find a way of getting the Bible without being seen, to look up the part that Mr. Van der Hoek had read in Sunday school. Could it really be true that her name was used there? She couldn't find it and didn't dare ask anyone. By the end of the day she had come down with a fever. At least that's what her mother thought. It was true Ika's cheeks glowed with a crimson flush, and that she had to clench her teeth together to stop them from chattering. But was it in fact a high temperature?

Later when she had been lying in bed awhile, she knew it wasn't a high temperature but the result of holding in her tears. For after her pillow had become wet, she calmed down slowly, though it still felt very strange to be crying on her birthday after she'd looked forward to it for such a long, long time.

When Simone returned it was already late in the afternoon. Ika had just settled down to work on a design for laying out the area surrounding the Promenade Hotel. There was to be a patio and a covered winter garden. It wasn't certain yet that they would get the commission. Simone sometimes tried to drive too hard a bargain, and she certainly didn't have much patience either. Therefore, it was Ika that did most of the consultations.

Ika hoped that Simone would carry off the deal. It would be a nice showpiece for their company. Offices and organizations that wanted to bring a little of nature indoors in a responsible way certainly got the right people in them. Berger's Landscape Gardening not only worked out the layout but also the maintenance. The business was going well, but so far they hadn't yet secured any big commissions. The Promenade Hotel would be a challenge.

Already Ika had various designs formulating in her head for the winter garden. Simone looked after the technical, commercial, and financial side of things, while Ika began work drawing up the plans and choosing the special plants. It was a division of labor that suited them both quite nicely.

Ika often had a feeling that she and Simone were business partners, although according to the books, Ika was but an employee. Perhaps it was like this because they'd also become friends over the ten years that Ika had worked for Berger's Landscape Gardening.

Ika burst out laughing when Simone stormed in. The joy at getting the work was written all over her broad face, so she didn't need to ask.

"We've got it!" Simone dropped her full weight onto the chair, kicked off her smart-looking shoes, and swung her feet to a nearby table. She nodded and said, "For the first time in our existence we're doing well, girl. It's at least six months worth of work for the boys. We can also do the paving."

"Did the discussion go all right?" asked Ika, still curious.

Simone grinned. "It's all wrapped up. It will be my treat at the Chinese restaurant this evening. When all's said and done, it was your idea to put out feelers there. Well, folks, we've landed the big one!"

Ika smiled weakly at the mention of the restaurant. "I'd rather not today, thanks."

"So your headache hasn't gone yet?"

Ika carefully shook her head in response.

"Have you phoned the doctor about your mother?"

"Yes, and it really is serious. He gives her three months at the most."

Simone stood up and paced the room. The friendly face of a few minutes before was now set in hard lines. It was as if Ika had to climb a thousand steps before she could make herself say it. And at the thousandth step, she would say that she was going.

Being awake at night wasn't the worst thing. What was bad was when she had to get to the bathroom. Ika was scared of the stairs, and the toilet was downstairs. The landing was all right, for the night-light was burning there. But the stairs felt like a dark pit, with shadows at the top from whatever had been left hanging over the banister. There was a pair of Father's pants and an apron of Mother's. The pant legs were long and the apron had ties that could entangle her like ropes. And the cold granite floor of the corridor—which made Ika feel like she was stepping into freezing water—sent shivers down her spine.

With her hand on the banister, Ika walked cautiously down the stairs. She knew there were fourteen steps. She always counted. In her mind she was singing a line out of the verse from the Psalms for the week. It was her experience that a person should always think about something else when afraid. Or pretend that it was all nothing. Then there was no need to be scared. She reminded herself that the hall was the same at night as it was in the daytime.

Mr. Molenaar the teacher said that one could always pray if frightened. So halfway down the stairs Ika had to get down on her knees suddenly, otherwise something might go wrong. Still, turning her back to all that awful darkness felt terrible.

How many steps had she done now? Was she there yet? She missed the last step and fell into the dark icy hallway. Ika knew that she shouldn't scream and with great effort she managed to bite back a shout, momentarily forgetting that she had to go to the bathroom. There was a warm trickle down her legs as she flew up the stairs again.

But before she reached her bed, her body had gone as cold as the feeling that gradually overcame her. Ika had wet herself, just like that, in the hall. And what would she do with those wet panties?

Simone was standing quietly at the window. She was moving her fingers as if drumming on the windowpane, but there was no sound.

Ika pushed her work away from her, as she had to make room. Then she said, "Can you imagine. . . ?"

Before Ika could finish her thought, Simone nodded and said, "For goodness' sake, don't do anything you'll be sorry for later."

Ika went and stood beside her. She would have loved to throw her arms around Simone, but that wouldn't have been the right thing with her. A slap on the shoulder was the usual thing, though such a gesture hardly suited the occasion. Instead, Ika laid her forehead on Simone's shoulder, resting there for a moment before she said, "I'm so scared . . . the minute I step into that house . . . that everything will overwhelm me."

Simone shrugged her shoulders, as much to avoid the words as the show of affection. "You may well be scared, but there are two things they can't talk to you about—guilt and blame. You've certainly paid your share of those by now, whether or not you deserved it. If anybody needed to make the sacrifice, you've done it."

In a few steps she was at her desk, emptying out her handbag. She'd never come right out with it. Yet Ika knew that, whatever happened, Simone was behind her.

She ought to go, but when, she wasn't sure. First, the most obvious need was to soothe away the flames behind her eyes, the violent drilling in her skull, with darkness and rest. Simone must have understood this, too, for without a word she went and picked up Ika's coat and rattled her car keys.

## CHAPTER FOUR

IKA WOKE UP with a feeling of surprise. It must still be early. In her bedroom there was already a soft white light. Outside no sound but that of the birds could be heard. The surprise was connected with a dream. The sounds of the birds too.

Far away a dove cooed, and then she remembered.

She moved her head carefully as she turned her face from side to side. After an attack like yesterday's, Ika had to test how much she could stand. Sometimes the monster seemed to be lurking somewhere behind her ear or lower in the muscles of her neck.

The dove cooed again. She threw back the quilt and sat up. The wave of nausea didn't come, so she got out of bed.

In front of the open window she thought about the dream.

Ika was at home. Mother was sitting at the table, peeling pears. The turtledove in his wooden cage hanging over the door in the hall seemed to be laughing. Mother laughed back. She could imitate the dove's sound exactly. The bird bowed and cooed. Mother could also imitate the cooing sound. It was as if the two of them were having a conversation.

She'd looked at Mother's raised face, at her mouth, as she said over and over again, "Coo-coo." Her mother appeared to be kissing the air.

It was a dream that could have been reality. Perhaps she'd really seen it just like this before and had hidden it away in her mind until now. Perhaps the pain of yesterday had brought it back to the surface, fished out of the sea of memories.

This was good. Mother talking to the dove. And above all, Mother's mouth. It was a beautiful mouth, as she remembered it. Mother's mouth could all at once bring a look of tenderness to her serious face. It was a small mouth, usually tight-lipped. Sometimes the corners turned up and disappeared into the thin folds of her cheeks. What would Mother look like now? What did anyone look like who was incurably ill, who had but a short time to live?

Ika couldn't imagine her mother any other way than how she had been in the dream. Her uplifted face as she sat at the table, her hands turned brown from peeling pears.

Could the dove still be alive? It might well be possible. Turtledoves could reach a ripe old age. It was actually her dove. Ika breathed in deeply the fresh morning air before closing and locking the window.

She would go this afternoon—that is, if Simone agreed for her to take the time off.

Granddad on her father's side had a farm. Ika loved going there, even though Granddad was a quiet man and Granny was long since dead. Ika went there mostly to see Aaltje, the elderly maid. Ika thought Aaltje was nice.

And Aaltje was always pleased when she came. Ika could see it in her eyes and by the way she always poured a glass of milk for her right away. Sometimes the milk was still warm. "You can't get fresher than that!" Aaltje would say, setting down the beaker in front of Ika on the table with its red-checkered oilcloth.

In truth Ika wasn't fond of milk still warm from the cow, but because Aaltje was watching her, she pretended to enjoy it.

"We've got young turtledoves," Aaltje said one day, "in the chestnut tree in front of the house."

"Can I go and see?" Ika asked.

"Oh, you won't see them. They're too high up. But if you listen, you can hear them. They're starting to cheep now."

Ika ran out to the chestnut tree at once. The tree was huge and very dense. Ika thought it was a beautiful tree. There was only one tree lovelier, and that was the old pear tree, whose branches hung over the shed.

Ika looked up, her head cocked to one side to listen better. She heard nothing and so wrapped her arms around the tree's trunk and listened with her ear against the bark.

She could hear a cow coughing from the cowshed and, farther away, the rattle of a train. She also detected the wind that was whistling among the branches, and a piece of canvas flapping somewhere. And Aaltje sang on about the winds and the waves, and how they obeyed the God who fed the birds.

Ika listened intently to the resounding notes.

"All good gifts around us
Are sent from heaven above.
So thank the Lord, O thank the Lord,
For all His love!"

*All good gifts.* It was beautiful. This was all about the young doves, and the hymn that they'd sung in Miss De Wit's class:

God who made the earth,
The air, the sky, the sea,
Who gave the light its birth,
Careth for me.

Ika wanted to sing but couldn't just now, because she had to wait for the young turtledoves' cheeping. Still, she couldn't keep the short verse from echoing in her ears.

Suddenly her grandfather was standing beside her. He must have had his slippers on, for she would certainly have heard him coming if he'd been wearing his clogs.

"What are ya doin'?"

"Listening out for the turtledoves, Granddad, but I can't hear them."

"At the front, above the fence."

Granddad walked with her and pointed to the nest within the branches. It took a while for Ika to find it. Then just as Granddad was turning around, she heard the cheeping, yet it had come from the ground. Among some withered leaves lay a young dove—bald and terribly ugly.

Soon the bird was nestled in Granddad's hand. Ika couldn't imagine it would later become a smooth, soft dove.

"Pushed out of the nest . . ." Granddad said.

"But why ever . . . ?"

Granddad shrugged his shoulders and said, "I'll have to finish it off, before the cat—"

"Oh, Granddad, may I keep it?"

He set the dove in her cupped hands. Ika never thought Granddad could be so careful.

"Give him old bread, a little milk, and later on some seed," he said.

The whole way home Ika was scared her mother wouldn't approve of her keeping the dove. Mother didn't like pets.

The tiny bird wriggled in her hands. She took a good look at him. How strange were his eyes, reddish blue under the thin layer of skin. "Quiet, now, quiet," she kept on saying to the baby dove and to her own fear.

Ika was amazed as the memories came back to her. She knew precisely how Mother had looked, as she had stood there in front of her so scared. And yet she'd somehow slowly and bravely raised her hands so that her mother could see just how pitiful the little bird was.

"Pushed out of its nest . . . without any warning . . . over the edge, falling to the ground . . ."

Ika had placed all her sympathy and indignation into those few words. Then like a warm spring tide came her joy at her mother's answer. "I think there's still an old dovecote in the shed."

How could she have forgotten that moment for so long? It was nothing short of a miracle. She would talk about it to Mother. Not only about all the other things, but about the dove, too, and why Mother had thought it was a good idea. Suddenly this seemed the most important thing of the moment.

"Oh, Lord, if only that dove were still alive."

That afternoon the meadows lay full-blown in the sun. The beech trees along the country road were all golden. The storm had wreaked havoc here as well. Many branches were scattered about on the road. The grass along the borders remained long, and the cows bent their heads low over the hedge to bite off the juiciest bits of green.

How beautiful it all was. Ika's heart felt as if it would burst. Dramatic changes had been made to the village. There was a completely new housing development. And the village streets were now lined with various boutiques and supermarkets.

She thought about buying flowers, but for some reason it didn't seem a good idea. Ika parked the car at the other end of the street, their street, only now with new trees and a little square where the old playground had been. She would walk slowly from there.

There weren't any new buildings really, and their house was still the last one. But the meadow behind it had been turned into an arrangement of lots. It was a good thing Father hadn't seen this. Or had he? How strange it was that she knew nothing about the previous fifteen years concerning her family. For the first time, Ika wondered why she hadn't responded to the card about Father's funeral. She had been away four years by that time. Perhaps she should have gone for the sake of Mother and Nelly.

She jumped when she heard the loud bell of a passing mobile

shop. It stopped at the house, then rang its bell again. The neighbor brushed by her, shouting from a distance to the milkman who was leaning out of his van to take her empty bottles. Ika walked on. She couldn't ring the doorbell now, not with the neighbor and milkman looking at her.

After she'd strode past the house she heard footsteps on the gravel path. A quick glance behind her told her it was Nelly—different, yet unmistakably her. When she said hello to the neighbor, Ika recognized her voice as well. Before Ika could plan what to do next, she was already on her way, walking around the back. She found the kitchen door open, and stepped inside.

The smell of the house overwhelmed her. The granite draining board, the gas range, the coconut matting, and the storage jars in the cupboard—everything appeared as it was fifteen years before. The dishcloth was still an old piece of vest. She clutched the tea towel and pressed her face into it. It smelled of the wind and the sun and the iron. With the tea towel still in her hand, Ika continued on up the two steps to the room.

The daylight was made dim, as the shutters were closed tight against the sun. On top of the chimneypiece, the clock was ticking emphatically. The plush tablecloth no longer had a plastic covering on it, and there were new wooden chairs.

Ika's eyes strayed to the sliding doors leading to the front room. Mother would surely be lying in there. She walked over to the doors, noticing that their leaded glass panels rattled. When she was young she could always tell by listening if a grown-up was approaching. If she was doing her homework in the front room, then she knew whether or not she should hide the library book between her school books.

Now the glass panes were rattling at her footsteps. They'd never done that before.

The sliding doors only needed to be opened a little way. The bed had been moved next to the window and placed on blocks. Ika sank down quietly into the chair in the corner.

Mother was sleeping. Her head lay a little crooked on the pillows, her right hand palm down on top of the sheet. Her face had gotten smaller. The cheeks had sunk in, and the eyelids looked transparent. But it was still Mother. The mouth hung slightly open. Ika could hear the strained breathing. Her hair lay beside her face in a single narrow braid, almost white now.

The sheets betrayed the contour of her mother's body. She must be thin, very thin indeed.

A bedpan had been placed under the bed. On the bedside table sat a beaker and a half-full glass of water. Ika's eyes picked out a drawing pinned onto the wallpaper over the bed. It was a child's drawing of a woman in bed with a broad grin on her face. The artist had written "For Granny, from Dirk-Willem" at the bottom. Pinned on the wallpaper! This showed how much she thought of it.

Through the thin curtains Ika saw the neighbor and Nelly as they walked toward the house from where the mobile shop had been parked. The neighbor shook her head pityingly when Nelly told her how she'd been so restless the whole night.

"Willem never got a wink of sleep. He was exhausted this morning. Mother kept needing to get out of bed to go to the toilet, but she can't stand on her legs. Of course, she didn't want a man to help her. So I'll be with her the whole day."

Nelly's voice grew plaintive. Soon the neighbor changed the subject to her sewing machine and it not working properly. Nelly seemed to understand such things. The neighbor then asked if she'd be able to come with her, to take a look at the machine.

Nelly nodded. She'd become plump since marrying. It was mostly her hips that had broadened, or was it because of the pleated skirt that she wore? Nelly's hair remained her greatest attraction. She now had it pushed up into a loose roll at the back of her head. Yet the tight little curls that encircled her face were arranged just as when she'd last seen her. She reminded Ika of a contented house cat. And she had lipstick on, which was something that surprised Ika.

Ika had been so busy staring at Nelly's outward appearance that she hadn't heard what Nelly was telling the neighbor. She was coming around the back now. Ika heard the milk bottles clanking as Nelly set them down on the kitchen counter. Then the panes on the sliding door trembled, and the footsteps halted. Ika could see that Nelly was looking down at Mother through the chink in the door.

Ika held her breath. The footsteps disappeared, and then a little later, Ika heard the neighbor's door shutting. Slowly Ika breathed out again, yet she held perfectly still. As she turned her attention from the sliding doors she noticed that Mother had her eyes open.

What was wrong with Mother's eyes that they stared at her like this? For there was no change, no recognition. A heavy silence pervaded the room, weighing down on Ika's shoulders. Her mother held a wasting look, one that lacked shock or any emotion at seeing her after fifteen years. It was as if her mother had known she'd be sitting there this day, this hour. As if Ika had been at her bedside the day before too. The silent staring seemed to put time on hold. Ika knew the blue-gray eyes as they had always been—red and bloodshot.

Ages had to be bridged. Mountains of anxiety, ravines of pain, depths of loneliness. Ika felt as if they were drifting together in the soundless universe, where the whole body consisted of one eye, and vision had crippled all other senses.

The clock's striking summoned time back, and Mother's hand—the one that was laying on the sheet—moved. Ika was at last able to take her eyes off Mother's and look at the hand. At first the hand appeared relaxed, but then it began grasping spasmodically at the sheet, as if her mother had just realized who was sitting beside her.

Then the hand transformed into the hand from long ago, the hand that had smacked her, that seized her by the shoulder. The hand that pointed at her and tapped accusingly on the partly steamed-up window.

A sudden panic overwhelmed her. With a jerk, Ika pushed the

chair back and fled through the sliding doors, then through the back door and across the street. Nauseated and gasping for air, she finally began to calm down within the enclosed space of her car. Only then did she realize that her running away had coincided with when she'd heard the dove calling.

"What's that dove doing here?" Father had asked when he came home in the evening.

Ika felt the color drain from her cheeks. Unsure of what to say, she looked to Mother. If Mother would only say something!

Instead, Nelly had launched into telling the entire story. Ika even convinced her about the pitifulness of the situation. Nelly had helped to find the cage, while Mother sat and waited with the dove on her lap. No, she hadn't wanted to hold him, but Ika was allowed to set the wee bird on her apron, in the warm hollow of her lap.

Ika had had to swallow hard, because she wanted to hug Mother tightly and stroke her face for being so kind. The cage had been stored at the back of a high shelf, and Nelly thought only Father would be able to reach it. But Ika was scared the whole thing wouldn't happen if Father had to be put out in any way. Earlier Ika had decided that, before Father came home, the dove would have to be safe and happy in his little cage. Father must see it was possible, and that Mother had already made up her mind about keeping the dove.

Therefore, at the risk of breaking her neck, Ika managed to climb up and retrieve the cage. It was dirty and covered with cobwebs. Mother had told her how to clean it. Meanwhile, Nelly fetched some newspaper to line the cage's floor.

In the center of the cage Ika placed an old piece of buttered bread and a little milk, and then carefully picked up the dove off her mother's lap to put him in the cage beside the food. With her eyes gleaming, Ika said, "Just feel, Mother, he's got warm through and through from you."

But her mother didn't care to feel the dove. "He's surviving well" was all she said.

Nelly's telling of the story passed over Ika's head. She was too preoccupied with studying the expression on her father's face. What would he say?

He'd spluttered something in disagreement, but nothing serious. This was most likely due to Nelly being the one to tell the story. For when Nelly spoke, her cute perfect ringlets danced with the shaking and nodding of her head.

"What do you think?" Father asked, glancing at Mother.

Mother shrugged her shoulders as her eyes wandered over toward Ika. But she was looking at Nelly when she said, "The child would be so pleased."

Knowing for certain that Mother had deliberately been vague about which child would be pleased had left Ika in such a dither she wasn't able to eat that evening. She had a secret with Mother.

As Ika started up the car, she realized she had another secret with Mother.

IKA NEEDED THREE more days. One day to make her decision, one to explain everything to Simone, and another to sort out all her work.

The first day was a Saturday. Rather than sleeping in, Ika lay looking up at the ceiling. Her instinctive feeling told her: "It's the only way."

This was different from the time with Father. She hadn't been involved then, but was able to set it aside with other matters that had been dealt with. Even when she'd received the wedding invitation from Nelly, she felt no great compulsion to respond. Anyway, she wouldn't have contributed anything to the event. She probably would have been a nuisance.

With Mother it was different. She'd cursed Mother the most, yet had also loved her the most. Throughout the years her reproach had been concentrated on Mother, although Ika had also tried to find a viable reason to excuse her. But she hadn't found a way to put Mother on the same side with the things of the past. Somehow she and her mother would walk the last bit of the path together.

Ika was scared as she pondered what she expected of that day. Did she really think that everything came out all right on a person's deathbed? What would happen to her if the task she'd taken on proved too difficult? Had she still more stairs to climb? Must she go even deeper? Was she only doing this to reassure herself that she'd done everything in her power to do? Did she need to convince herself that she wasn't to blame for anything? But would Mother want to talk now? Would she finally break her silence after all these years and tell Ika who her father was?

And how would it go with Nelly? Or with all the others she'd see again after so much time having gone by, such as the minister, church elders, and family members who would be sure to be visiting? It all seemed insurmountable to her. Questions would be fired at her: "Ika, where have you been? Where do you live now? What do you do? Why?" She already knew how people would look at her, how they would assess what she had achieved. They'd be curious about her personal life and disparage her appearance. The narrow-mindedness of the whole village would flood over her.

It was for this reason that she wanted to take work with her, so that she could legitimately duck out of seeing people she didn't particularly like. It would help if now and then she could get back to the familiar, to the work she loved. A task she could creep away into, such as making something beautiful of the winter garden and patio of the Promenade Hotel. She had to have something for herself, tied to the present, so as not to drown in the sea of the past. The contact with Simone would protect her against ending up in her earlier anxiety. She'd have to keep reminding herself that her flight had taken place years ago and that she had since created her own way of life. Simone would be her anchor. This was the upshot of the first day.

The Whitsun market. Getting up early and being out and about as early as six o'clock. Shivering with the cold and excitement, rattling the change so carefully saved up and Granddad's guilders. Ika looked forward to it days ahead, especially when she rounded the corner of Bree Street and caught sight of the square in front of the town hall. Rows and rows of flowers, garden supplies, vegetables, houseplants, and giant ferns.

Nelly walked beside her. Father and Mother would come a little later, then afterward they'd all go to church.

Ika hoped that the big truck would be there again with the salesman who shouted with his booming voice, who brought the most beautiful plants for people to buy. Ika loved listening to him. He always said the same thing, but in different words. He'd start with one plant for a guilder and twenty-five cents, then throw in another just because he was in a good mood, and then another because of the pleasant weather. Sometimes yet another plant, because it was supposed to rain the next day. It was all nonsense, but got things sold nonetheless. Ika thought him to be the best salesman in the world. He made sure everyone went home with their arms full.

"Come on now, Nelly, let's do this one first," Ika insisted as Nelly began to lag behind.

"I'm cold," Nelly said, trembling. "Aren't Father and Mother coming soon?"

Ika gave a quick nod while pulling her along. She had discovered a stall full of different cacti. Mother loved them because they were so easy to care for. Perhaps she should buy a small one for Mother. But she couldn't decide till she'd seen everything.

They then stopped at the bedding plants. Ika hadn't intended to buy anything, but the bright yellow sunflowers that looked like little suns seemed to call out to her. On thin stems above the fresh green foliage with minute serrated edges, their cheery faces were waving in the breeze.

While Ika stood mesmerized by the bobbing plants, Nelly had strolled on alone. She'd forgotten to tell Nelly to wait. Ika had become absorbed in imagining a little garden of her own, using the piece of earth near the shed, the place where the plant she knew as Judas penning was growing. If Father would allow it, then she could look after the garden by herself. A little bit of ground for herself. She'd also get a few bean plants to climb up against the shed. Or maybe tomatoes or radishes. The idea offered so many possibilities that her heart began beating faster.

"*Doronicum caucasicum*," said the boy beside her. Ika looked up, startled. He nodded and stood looking like a real market tradesman, with his hands in his pockets, summing her up.

"Pardon?" Ika said, all the while rattling her money, so that he'd know she had some.

"*Doronicum caucasicum*. Most people call them spring sunflowers."

She repeated these magic words to herself. They so suited the waving sunny faces. She took all her money out of her coat pocket and gave it to him. He counted it and stroked his hair from his eyes.

"Is it not enough?" she asked tensely.

"Depends. How many do you want?" He had to laugh at the relief in her face. Suddenly he said, "I know you. You've been over to the farm where Aaltje is. I live on Heren Street too. The nursery further up is my father's." He pointed with his thumb over his shoulder toward a big blond man who was settling up with a customer. Then the boy rolled up the plant skillfully in a newspaper and said, "It's a perennial. It comes up again every year by itself."

"Do you know all the names?" Ika wanted to know.

He nodded as if it was nothing. "Yeah, I hear them all the time. It's no big deal."

"I'm going to make my own little garden!" Ika exclaimed.

"Well, just pop in and see us anytime. We've got everything you need to make yourself a nice garden."

In a state of wonderment, Ika went to look for Nelly, who was now hopping along between Father and Mother. Father's eyes looked dark and contorted. "You call that looking after your sister!"

Ika decided it would be better to hold off on her question about the garden until later, when Father might be in a better mood. To make everything all right again she bought a cactus for Mother and a cinnamon stick for Nelly, which, together with her spring sunflower, had meant spending all her money. On their way home to get ready for church, Ika smiled as she glanced down at the little suns nodding their heads with every step she took, in time to their name, *Doronicum caucasicum.*

During the church service, Ika designed her first garden. It was barely two square yards, but in her mind it was as big and beautiful as the paradise the minister had preached about.

With Simone, Ika's decision became more difficult. Ika phoned her from bed on Sunday morning.

"Can I maybe come over today?" Ika asked more timidly than usual.

Simone didn't seem exactly sympathetic. "On Sunday afternoon? It must be urgent."

"It is, yes."

"Is she dead, then?"

"No, but can we talk about it this afternoon?"

"Then we'll come to blows!" Simone said and slammed down the receiver.

Ika must have practiced ten times how she'd tell her, yet still hadn't felt any better about it. A quarrel with Simone was the last thing she could stand in this situation.

By the time she rang Simone's bell at two-thirty, Ika had forgotten all her arguments. Simone let her in silently and then led the way into the living room.

As always, Ika was impressed by Simone's house. It was exceptionally simple—sparsely furnished but warm. Whoever came into Simone's house saw into her soul, which was the reason she entertained very few people.

The brown Chesterfield sofa was the only large piece of furniture in the main room. And the single painting that dominated the room was the glass wall overlooking a spectacular garden.

Folding her arms across her chest, Simone sank into the wicker chair, which creaked loudly under her weight. Ika sat down on the sofa opposite Simone and clasped her hands on her lap. She could tell that Simone understood. After all, they had only each other.

Their time began with just the silent looking, when the eyes appeared to have started the impending battle.

Since Ika remained quiet, Simone finally said, "Why should you do it? Can you give me one argument why you should go and nurse your mother? Are you really intending to undo all those years of breaking free for the sake of a sentimental letter that begins, 'My dear Ika'?"

Ika went over and looked through the glass into the garden, where the deep purple of the autumn asters could be seen in profusion. A bird was drinking at the pond. All was silent, and so her ears picked up the faint splashing sound of the fountain outside. She suddenly had the feeling her head was coming loose from her body and had begun to glide around the room. Her ears were ringing, and a white haze rose up in the four corners of the room.

A cold, wet washcloth brought her to her senses again. Ika was lying on the floor, with Simone's eyes just above her. When the room stood still again she suddenly had to laugh at the sight of Simone pouring still more water from a flower vase on the washcloth.

"Go on, laugh, you rotten girl. You scared me silly!"

Soon Ika's laughter turned to crying, and Simone, who almost never cried, started to weep too. A little while later, they were laughing together again, this time at the spectacle of their blubbering.

Then Simone gave her a well-meaning thump on the thigh and helped her up onto the sofa. "You rotten girl," she said again as she stepped over to the table and commenced pouring out two sizable glasses of port.

When Simone set it down in front of her, Ika felt a strange fear surrounding the glass. Simone emptied hers in a few gulps, but Ika didn't need the port any longer. She wanted to talk without anything clouding her thinking or sapping her strength.

It was Simone who started it up again, resuming their former conversation by asking the question, "Do you really want to know who your father was?"

It had been a winter's afternoon. At four o'clock, dusk had already fallen. Ika was in the second class of the junior school, or the HBS. As usual the bus home was overfull. She had to push and shove and shift her book bag in front of her across the bus's floor. The driver kept trying to cram in more people at every stop, shouting for them to walk to the back of the bus, though there wasn't any room there. Ika gathered the nerve, then pushed into the crowd of people. She didn't like standing at the back, because this was where the boys from the technical school were. She was still afraid of them, even though they had quit bullying her since she'd left the village school. Yet somewhere deep within her lurked the suspicion that these boys could be more dangerous than ever before. She finally obeyed the grumpy voice of the driver calling for her and some others to move toward the back of the bus.

Before Ika knew it she was standing pressed up against a seat and the body of another person. A huge boy, though he probably wasn't much older than she was. Directly in front of her, she could see his chin with a few solitary hairs sprouting from it. He was speaking to somebody toward the front. She felt his breath in her hair and the moving of his diaphragm as he yelled to his friend several seats away. She began to breathe through her mouth because she found his body odor unpleasant. Ika had the feeling of being crushed, for he was leaning more and more heavily on her. At each corner of the road she could feel his body flattening her. Of course, he didn't do anything improper and probably had no idea that Ika felt she was suffocating because of him. But at the next stop she broke away from the boy, clawing and fighting her way through the surprised people till finally escaping out the front exit.

The bus left her in the middle of the countryside. She still had another hour to get home, yet anything was better at that moment than the nearness of the boy on the bus.

When Ika arrived home much later than normal, clearly tired with her heavy bag on her back, there was a surprise waiting for her. Mother had been standing at the door—something that hadn't happened before—and her face was white as a sheet. Her relief could be heard above her anger.

Ika found that she couldn't say why she had left the bus. Mother thought that she'd been irresponsible to go walking alone on that isolated country road like she did. This was asking for trouble. Had they bought her an expensive bus pass just to get off in the middle of the route for no good reason? And who would have to tell Father if some mean fellow had done goodness knows what to her?

Ika had put up with Mother's hand that had shaken her thoroughly, because Mother had been standing waiting at the door—as white as a sheet, with such worry in her eyes.

Ika shrugged her shoulders. "I don't know if it will make any difference, but I'd just like her to tell me. If it happened that she was raped, of course I won't go looking for the fellow. And you won't see me on the doorstep of some happily married couple either, to ruin the man's life with the fact that I might be his daughter. But she has to tell me. It doesn't matter who it is . . . I just want to know."

Simone nodded and then poured more port for herself.

Ika had become tired and distressed, so Simone couldn't persuade her to accompany her to the Chinese restaurant that evening. Ika wouldn't hear of it. Perhaps because never before had she eaten out on a Sunday.

The third day was a Monday. Although nothing had been arranged between Simone and Ika, it was quite normal that Ika should take the work for the Promenade Hotel with her along with all the materials she might need: the smaller drawing board, technical pens and colored pencils, the lists of plants, catalogs, and reference books. It was all a load, but every extra pound made her more aware of the importance of her present situation, of her friendship with Simone.

Around five P.M., Simone waved good-bye to her from the window as Ika was leaving. She about filled the entire opening with her gesturing. Ika wondered if the filing cabinet near the window had taken another beating and Simone had broken her toes once again.

"If you haven't phoned me by the end of the week, I'll come in person and fetch you!" was the last threat Simone had shouted. It was a heartwarming threat.

## CHAPTER SIX

WATCHING AND PRAYING. This was all Ika did during the night between Monday and Tuesday. She opened the little Bible she got when she left Sunday school, looking for the text she had to learn when she had discovered her name's origin on her birthday. She still remembered the text, yet didn't know where to find it. Now she wanted to know what else was there. It seemed to be important. "Remember ye not the former things, neither consider the things of old. Behold, I will do a new thing; now it shall spring forth; shall ye not know it? I will even make a way in the wilderness, and rivers in the desert." If only God would do this. Make a way for her in the wilderness, a river in the desert. If only she could reach the point where the old things faded away and she could believe in something new. However close the friendship was to her, it became clear that Simone wasn't a strong enough anchor.

Ika didn't feel like waiting any longer, so she got up at first light. When she drove into the village the streets were populated with children on their way to school. Running and shouting, they paid no attention to the traffic, and Ika had to apply the brakes repeatedly. The children looked at her with blank expressions on their faces. Would Nelly's boys be among them? Was she hoping to recognize something in a child's face? Giving in to the impulse to delay her purpose, Ika drove on to her old school.

She parked the car a little distance away, then walked over to take a peek at the students, who seemed already to be engrossed in their studies, many in daydreaming. Ika noticed that there had been classrooms added on, but the main hall remained the same and the gymnasium too. Her not recognizing a single adult—some busy inside the school, others acting as supervisors on the playground—was a disappointment to her. But she should have known that she couldn't expect to see Mr. Molenaar or Miss Toms.

When Mr. Molenaar cried, something would happen to the class. For everyone had the feeling they were witnessing an event that they maybe shouldn't be. He only cried when he spoke of the New Heaven and the New Earth. But the crying didn't prevent him from continuing to tell the story through to its end, and Ika could recall the image of his speaking with a drip hanging from his chin. She used to watch the tear as it slipped out of the corner of his eye, traced its way down to his stubbly chin, and finally became a round dark blot on his gray shirt.

Nobody dared to make fun of him, not even afterward, because

Mr. Molenaar told stories so beautifully. It was more like painting than telling stories, Ika had thought, because she could see it all in front of her eyes in the finest of detail.

"Some day everything will become new, boys and girls. Oh, I thank God that I may know He will make everything new!" This was always his last sentence, after which he'd turn his back to the class and blow his nose noisily. Then he was himself again. Mr. Molenaar, a teacher who could take a joke and even sometimes be outright ridiculed. But on the days he cried the class would be seized with a peculiar respect, a sort of reverence.

Once Mr. Molenaar had to go before the school board, because they questioned whether his teaching was sound. Somebody had complained that the teacher never spoke of sin and guilt. The whole school knew about the meeting. Such gossip traveled fast in the village. The strongest boys carried chairs up the stairs to the classroom for those on the school board, which consisted of four men in black suits, all smoking cigars.

Ika recognized the board members. These were the very same men who sat in the church council section at the front of her church. Their heavy voices and bodies turned the students into pale, motionless dolls. Ika was scared Mr. Molenaar would start to cry again when he did the Bible story, this time in front of the four dark-suited men sitting at the back of the classroom.

But it didn't happen. Probably because the story wasn't about the New Heaven and the New Earth but was about Naaman, the Syrian who went to Elisha, the man of God, to be cured of his leprosy. Mr. Molenaar told it well. Ika didn't dare to look, but the men behind her must have thought it was lovely, also, because they were so quiet.

After it was over Mr. Molenaar followed up with a few questions, something he often did to make sure they'd understood the general meaning of the story. "What precisely is a man of God?" he asked the class.

Ika put up her hand, and when he had nodded to her, she said, "Somebody like you, Mr. Molenaar!"

The teacher grew red in the face, and his lip trembled when he said, "I won't accept that answer, Ika. I think I'm more like Naaman, the leper."

Fortunately he didn't start to cry, though he blew his nose in the familiar way. The school board members then stood up. Ika sighed, as she was relieved to feel no longer their eyes piercing her back. Nor the teacher's eyes, which she had felt were on her that day.

The school bell woke Ika out of her reverie. The playground was empty, except for a solitary latecomer. She returned to her car and drove the familiar way that she previously used to walk to school. It now seemed hardly any distance at all.

Her old street was quiet. The early birds had flown off somewhere, and now everyone waited for their coffee and for the many shops to open.

Ika parked the car in front of the house and then walked over the gravel toward the back. She had expected to see Nelly, but when she stole a glance through the kitchen window, she saw instead a burly man standing at the sink, shaving. Ika was perplexed, and it took a moment for her to realize that this must be Willem, Nelly's husband. She'd prepared herself for everything, but not a confrontation with an almost unknown brother-in-law.

Her gasp of astonishment had attracted his attention, for he turned around with the shaving foam still on his cheek. He needed more time than she did, but then his reaction was surprisingly quick. He strode over and threw the kitchen door wide open.

"Well, would ya look at this, an early visitor!" When Ika didn't move, he beckoned her with his bare arm to step inside. "Come on in, the coffee's ready."

The kitchen didn't look like their kitchen anymore—not with Willem in it. He was the boss here, and that didn't tally with Ika's memory. In a jiffy he set the steaming cup of coffee in front of her, after making her take a seat at the table.

Then he resumed his shaving while continuing to talk. Ika couldn't recall him being so chatty. His broad back and the rippling muscles of his arms amazed her, as she thought of how this big strong man had grown out of the gawky boy of earlier days. A dab of shaving cream rolled down his thick neck onto his vest. It must have tickled him, for he gave the spot a smack with the flat of his hand. Now and then they had eye contact in the mirror that was once her father's. But Ika didn't need to say much, as Willem talked enough for the both of them.

She knew before he had finished shaving that Mother had had a bad night. The word *Mother* sounded very strange coming from Willem. He had also informed her that Mother had only fallen asleep a few hours before daybreak, and that since Friday, Mother had done nothing but call for her, call for Ika. They'd had a difficult time with her, he went on, because Mother kept insisting that she'd seen Ika and that Ika had gone away without saying anything. They eventually had to ask the doctor to give her an injection. There was no other way to calm her down. "So it's cool that you've come," Willem said.

*Perhaps "cool" wasn't the right word,* Ika thought, *but the boys probably used the word as a super-superlative so that would explain it.* And while Willem was rattling on like this, Ika could only think of one thing: *Nelly had certainly not made a bad choice with this man.*

"Should I phone Nelly and tell her you're here?" he said as he refilled her coffee cup without asking.

Ika shook her head. "I'd first like to be alone with Mother." Following the robust noise Willem had been making, her voice now sounded soft to herself.

"Okay then, I'll just say that to Nell. Can you manage things by yourself till about eleven o'clock?"

"Of course," Ika said.

After he had closed the back door behind him, the house grew deathly quiet.

Through the crack between the sliding doors Ika looked in on her mother. She was still asleep, her chest rising with silent regularity. Her face appeared sunken, more noticeably now than last week. The cheekbones could clearly be seen above the hollows where once her cheeks had been. Ika turned aside. She wanted no repetition of last Friday. This time she'd wait until Mother called.

Ika stroked the plush tablecloth against the pile. She had done the same action many times as a child, except when there was a plastic cover on top. She then glanced up at the dove above the door in the hallway. He looked at her from his perch and bowed a few times before cooing. Ika brought a chair over and climbed up on it. Pulling open the cage's little door slowly, she waited patiently till the dove jumped from his perch onto her hand. She lifted him out and held his soft body against her cheek. The dove was not afraid. He still remembered, as his heart beat against the palm of Ika's hand.

The clock struck nine. She was home. Ika set the dove down in the first patch of sunlight on the tablecloth. He immediately raised his wing so as to warm up the underside as well. It was as if he were hoisting a sail.

Father had eventually noticed that it was Ika's dove. It was so often on her shoulder. Mother hated it when the bird flew around in the house, and it seemed to understand this. So it came to be that the dove was allowed out of the cage only if he sat quietly with Ika.

One day in the spring Ika was standing in front of the window with the dove on her shoulder, when another dove in the pear tree began to call. Ika noticed by the trembling feathers that he recognized the call. He called back, and the dove in the pear tree answered again. Restlessly the dove flapped up to Ika's head, then flew off with a thud against the window. The dove fell and lay stunned on the windowsill.

Bewildered, Ika picked him up and placed him back in his cage where she stroked him with her hand. She kept looking at the window where a faint impression of his wings could still be seen. The dove on the pear tree kept on calling. The idea that her dove perhaps needed another dove to be happy shocked her. That he had wanted to fly away from her just because he'd heard another of his kind calling was a thought that hurt her.

"Don't I look after you well enough?" she whispered with tears in her eyes.

"Let that bird fly off!" her father said. "It's only logical that a bird like that wants his freedom. Do you want him always to sit in that cage?"

Mother just shrugged her shoulders. "First you'll move heaven and earth to keep the dove, and now you want to let him go! What sort of funny child are you? Is cleaning out the cage as bad as all that?"

But that was not the question here. For this didn't concern what *she* wanted, but what the dove wanted. Yet when she attempted to explain this to Mother, Mother wasn't willing to listen. "A dove can't want anything!" she had said.

Ika went to Granddad with the problem. Maybe he'd know the answer. Granddad was milking at the time, so she wasn't sure if he was really listening. It was quiet for a long time after she had finished talking. Granddad then carried the milk churn outside. He was the last farmer who still worked with churns, and all the milk not used for Aaltje's cheese making was sold from the house. Ika followed him, uncertain whether she should tell her story all over again.

But Granddad had indeed heard it. He leaned against the door of the cowshed, which was warm from the sun, and looked up toward the sky with screwed-up eyes as if he expected rain. "An animal learns from its parents not only where to find food but also how to protect himself against danger. He'd probably manage to find food, but you wouldn't want the cats to graze on him, would you?"

This was some speech from Granddad. While he talked he kept looking up at the sky. Ika studied him to see if he would say something more. He didn't. Instead he turned around and walked away.

Ika walked slowly home. She had completely forgotten to say hello to Aaltje. Once home she told the dove the difference between freedom and safety, and that life in a cage might not be so wonderful but it was a whole lot better than ending up in the claws of a cat. "But," she added, "I understand just what you feel."

With the dove against her cheek, Ika again went to the crack between the sliding doors. "Maybe you should have dared!" she whispered, her lips brushing his smooth feathers.

Time crept by. *It is strange that Mother should stay asleep so long,* Ika thought. She finally entered the room and leaned anxiously over the bed, listening to her mother's breathing, feeling her narrow wrist. Ika examined the medicine bottles and boxes that sat on the bedside table. Maybe Willem had given Mother a sleeping pill. But the names on the bottles didn't mean anything to her. *Should Mother be taking all these pills?* she wondered. Ika counted six different kinds.

Next to the medicine bottles was a Bible. Ika took it out with her to the table in the back room. She glanced down to where it fell open at the bookmark Nelly had made when in kindergarten. Colorful threads interlaced into a perforated card. Ika smiled because she still remembered how proud Nelly had been of it. The little bookmark had been between the pages of her mother's Bible for over twenty-five years. Mother had the habit of reading the Good Book from front to back and then starting all over again.

Every day her hand moved the bookmark forward page by page.

The Bible had opened where Mother had last stopped—Isaiah 43. Ika's eyes glazed over, as she was captivated by the ancient words. She decided to read the passage out loud. " 'But now thus saith the Lord that created thee, O Jacob, and he that formed thee, O Israel, Fear not: for I have redeemed thee, I have called thee by thy name; thou art mine. When thou passest through the waters, I will be with thee; and through the rivers, they shall not overflow thee: when thou walkest through the fire, thou shalt not be burned; neither shall the flame kindle upon thee. For I am the Lord thy God, the Holy One of Israel, thy Saviour . . . . ' "

As her eyes continued to pass over the lines, the quiet reading aloud became more of a whimper, for further on she found the part she'd been looking for. The text that admonishes not to think of previous things, and the promise that God would make something new, a way in the wilderness, rivers in the desert.

At one time she may have wavered between chance and guidance. This time it was nothing less than a touch. Ika laid her forehead on the pages.

Mother would have to wake up now.

## CHAPTER SEVEN

FOOTSTEPS THROUGH THE GRAVEL and the harsh sound of the doorbell brought Ika to her senses with a jolt. From between the sliding doors came Mother's voice, soft and a little hoarse. "Nelly, there's somebody at the door. Nelly!"

Ika stood up, not sure for a moment what to do first. She ran up to the sliding doors, but then at the last moment she thought better of it and so ran into the hall. With difficulty she unlocked the front door.

There stood a small plump woman on the step, whom Ika vaguely recognized. The woman smiled in a surprisingly sweet way and held out her hand. "How lovely to meet the eldest daughter here!"

The striking brows and the smell of disinfectant that lingered around her put Ika on the right track. It was Mrs. Wamers, the district nurse.

Briskly the nurse hung up her coat on the hallstand, and showing she knew her way around, proceeded to walk through the room. With a jolt she pushed the sliding doors wide open.

"Good morning, Mrs. de Haan. How are you today? I'm here nice and early. I'll give you a good wash first and then maybe I'll have time for a cup of coffee. That would be great, wouldn't it?"

Bustling around, she then fetched a basin from under the bed and grabbed two hand towels and a bath towel from out of the linen closet. With one flowing movement, which didn't fit with her plumpness, she set the basin in Ika's hands, turned to the bed again, and pulled the sheets and blankets away.

Ika stood in the doorway, overcome by the nurse's presence and her pace. And shocked that her mother had become so diminutive.

"Off you go, girl. Get the water! Not too warm. Just feel it with your elbow as if it was the bath water for a little child!"

While Ika was letting the hot and cold water mix in the basin she tried to recover herself. Despite the shock she'd just experienced, she filled the kettle right away for new coffee.

In the front room the easy chatter of the nurse went on for a while. When Ika set the water down on the table beside the bed, Mother was lying on the bath towel without any nightdress. Her hollow eyes, which now seemed too large, followed Ika wherever she went.

"It's great you have your eldest daughter with you, Mrs. de Haan. Now your other daughter can give a bit more attention to her own family. Is she going to stay for a while? She doesn't live around here, does she?"

While the nurse continued to talk, the narrow sunken body was expertly soaped. Ika didn't want to look, yet she couldn't tear her eyes away from what she saw. Fortunately the nurse was standing in front of her, so she didn't see everything. But the sticklike arms and the trembling legs shocked her, until somewhere deep in her chest the pain started.

The kettle whistled, signifying the coffee could now be made. When Ika had finished taking care of it, the nurse called.

"Can you come here, please? I'm going to show you how you should treat these bedsores."

Ika stepped timidly over to the bed. Mother was now lying on her stomach, her head half turned into the pillow. She looked depleted after her wash, for she panted and had her eyes closed.

The nurse pointed to the tender places. The skin, red and smarting, had shrunk back and was surrounded by thin, almost transparent skin that couldn't bear the fold in the sheet any longer.

Ika felt a wave of nausea come over her, but stayed put nonetheless and saw how the nurse carefully swabbed the open places with special tissues and then dried them with a compact hair-dryer.

It hurt her. Ika could see this from the spasm that passed over Mother's body. Finally she couldn't stand it any longer and ran away. Standing over the sink, she was barely able to gulp down the rising nausea. How would she make herself treat Mother's sores?

Ika returned when Mother was sitting up a bit higher against the pillows with a clean nightie on. The nurse was doing her hair. "Can I pour the coffee now?"

The nurse answered that she could. Then Ika's eyes met her mother's. "Ika," Mother said, and an expression halfway between laughing and crying flitted across her face.

"Oh yes—Ika," the nurse repeated. "I knew your eldest daughter had a strange name. How did you come to think of that, Mrs. de Haan?"

Ika hurried into the kitchen to avoid the answer, but Mother didn't answer.

"She can't drink it too hot, you know," the nurse said as she took Mother's cup from the tray for her.

While they were sipping their coffee, the nurse struggled to think of memories they'd all have in common. In particular her youngest sister, Mary, seemed to have done well for herself. Mary was fifteen years younger than she and therefore the same age as Ika.

*Maybe she's talking so much, because I'm not saying anything,* Ika thought. Ika then looked over at Mother's cup of coffee on the bedside table. It should have cooled down enough by now. But she couldn't bring herself to help Mother. *Later, after the nurse has left.* For if Ika tried to do anything now, she'd just embarrass herself with her clumsy butterfingers.

One of Ika's earliest memories was of drinking coffee after church at Mother's parents' house. She had to call them Grandfather and Grandmother. As for Granddad, he was Father's father, a quite different situation. Ika liked going there. Aaltje was there.

At Grandfather and Grandmother's there was nothing. Only the dark room with high, upright chairs with ball feet. The ball feet were Ika's only diversion. She didn't talk, because children were to be seen and not heard, and she was frightened of Grandmother's eyes. To kill time she'd stroke her stockinged feet around the smooth polished curves of wood. This was a soothing feeling that distracted her from the heavy menacing voices that usually filled the room.

It seemed always to be busy at Grandfather's house. This was because of his being a minister in the church. There were people constantly calling for one thing or another, or wanting to discuss the sermon.

Grandfather would sit in a big leather chair. His eyes saw everything. And he insisted on beginning the conversation, which sometimes took a long time. So long in fact that everything about Ika began to prickle and itch and she felt she couldn't swallow.

It was a relief when Grandfather sighed at last and said, "Yes, yes, good folks. We couldn't save ourselves!" Then with his sharp eyes he'd look at everyone in turn, calling each by name. To her he said "Ikabod," to her father "Dirk," and invariably to Mother he said "My fallen daughter." And then he would glance at her again, and Mother seemed to grow smaller. At this moment, Ika thought her mother might crawl under the table.

Like Ika, Mother was afraid of Grandfather. Yet after the third cup of coffee, when they were about to leave, Mother still kissed

Grandfather, and he would place his large white minister's hand on her head. He expected Ika to kiss him good-bye also. She didn't have any fear over whether he'd put his hand on her head, because he never did. And it was years after Grandfather had died before Ika understood the reason why.

Nurse Wamers stood up. She still had more work to do. "I have a good solution," she said to Ika. "Just give your mother a straw, and then if you hold the cup steady, she can manage it herself."

Ika blushed at the contempt in Nurse Wamers's voice. Of course, she was somebody with experience and over the years had learned to read between the lines. *Lacking what it takes* was clearly to be seen in the nurse's eyes. Ika walked with Nurse Wamers to the door but didn't have a chance to get her coat.

The door clicked shut, and Ika turned and walked slowly down the always cold and gloomy hallway. The black of the granite floor had been carried over to the painted paneling, so that the hall resembled a dark canal with banks. Added to the effect of the watery floor were the narrow hall window and the glass panel in the front door, which held green and blue stained glass.

A shiver ran down Ika's spine.

The kitchen embraced her with the warmth of the early morning sunshine. The light had restored the plush tablecloth to its former glory and made a shaft of dancing dust flecks.

Ika leaned with her back against the door. This was the only room in the house she liked. But there was no time to stand around. The front room called her precisely because everything had remained so quiet there.

She rushed to the sliding doors. The tinkling of the glass panes went on for a long time, but was this because the hand Ika used to grasp the doorjamb trembled?

"There are some straws in the far left kitchen drawer," Mother said, her eyes on the coffee cup.

*I can't put it off any longer*, Ika thought as she walked with the straw into the front room. She sat down on the edge of the bed and waited for Mother to look at her, but Mother was shy and avoided eye contact.

"Lovely coffee," she said, when Ika dried her mouth with a hanky, in the corners where there were traces of the brown liquid.

Ika recognized the compliment and saw that her mother was doing her best to be pleasant and appreciative. "Hello, Mother," she said softly.

"You were here on Friday as well," said Mother, sinking with a sigh back into the pillows.

Ika nodded. But because Mother had closed her eyes, she said it once more, aloud. "Yes, I was here on Friday too."

"Why did you go away without saying anything?"

"I don't know. I was scared, I guess."

Mother's eyes opened. "Scared? Scared of what?"

Ika shrugged her shoulders. "Scared of everything here. Scared of the past."

Ꭽ

"You mustn't be scared," the boy with the blond hair and the candid eyes said. "It's because you're scared that there's danger. If you're not scared, there won't . . ."

Ika had been standing at the gate of the nursery but didn't dare to go any further, because there was a dog, a big black dog. She'd been standing there waiting indecisively for half an hour and was debating whether just to go to Granddad's farm, to Aaltje. And then from behind, she heard the abrupt brakes of a bike. It was the boy from the Whitsun market. From the way that his eyes lit up, Ika could see that he still recognized her.

"You can just walk on through."

Her eyes sped to the dog lying in the sun in front of the shed. The boy laughed and said the one sentence she was often to think of later: "It's because you're scared that there's danger. If you're not scared, there won't . . ." It contained a great ring of truth for Ika-bod, though she had never looked at it like this before.

The box with the plants was heavy, but it was an unaccustomed pleasure for her to carry it. She'd gotten so much from Bart. Yes, she now knew he was named Bart, for she had heard his father call for him one day.

"How's that *Doronicum?*" he asked.

Ika blushed. *Imagine him still remembering that,* she thought. She told him about the garden where formerly only Judas pennings grew, where now the shining faces of her *Doronicum caucasicum* were making a good show.

"But that's almost over now, you know," Bart said. "After the longest day, they don't bloom anymore. You'd better take some of these. It's called *Dicentra spectabilis.* The ordinary name is bleeding heart. They bloom right up to autumn."

He had found a cardboard box for her, as though she were a real customer, and then set some of the plants into it.

"I haven't got any money," Ika had warned him in a fearful voice. "I only came to look . . . like you said . . . that time at Whitsun."

He then stopped what he was doing and looked at her. How blue his eyes were.

"Who's talking about money? This isn't for business. This is my own affair. What's your name, anyway?"

The blood raced to her head when she said her name. She had never before thought it to be a more awful name than right then. "Ikabod." Oh, if only he didn't know the name was in the Bible.

"Ikabod?" he echoed inquiringly. "And in Dutch?"

A laugh had come into his eyes, and Ika had only shrugged out of sheer embarrassment.

She finally answered, "There is no Dutch word for it."

"I'll think up something, then," Bart said.

The whole way home Ika had mused over him being called Bart and that he'd said he would think up a Dutch name for her, and also what he'd said about being afraid. *It's because you're scared that there's danger.*

But could she manage not to be scared anymore?

 

With her eyes closed, Mother said, "You always were a worrier." Her voice sounded sad, but bitter too. "Why did you come here?"

"I'm not sure. Maybe from worry again."

"The past always comes back to you. We weren't born for ease, and there's a lot you still have to know."

"But I don't know if I want to," Ika said.

"It would be better if you didn't have to know it." Two tears fell from under the closed eyelids and traced a path over the sunken cheeks.

Ika clasped her hands together. She had to call Simone later. Her decision to come had certainly not proven to be a good one, for her or for Mother.

Ika stood up, and Mother suddenly opened her eyes. Ika was astonished by the pent-up strength and intensity that radiated from her eyes.

"You can't go yet. I've first got to tell you everything."

Ika nodded silently and tried to see what else was in Mother's eyes. This strength of will, this intensity, had to be nurtured from within.

Was Mother's peace of mind dependent on her attitude? Or did Mother want her to share in the hatred that had forever been there? Would she now finally hear the reason for the resistance that made Mother take refuge in sickness and seclusion? The incomprehensible, powerless defense against something or someone, yet not saying clearly what or who. Who then? What then? Father? Grandfather? The village?

Mother withdrew, white-faced, and Ika begged her to rest first. They would talk later.

"No, be quiet for now. I'm staying. I'll not go away," Ika assured her.

Only after she had pulled the sliding doors shut did she realize their first conversation had already taken place, though few words were said. Ika also realized she'd have to proceed cautiously, step by step. It gave her the feeling that again she was standing on the stairs, looking into the darkness of the hallway, that icy depth of black water into which she had to let herself drop and pass through.

Mother was away that evening, and Father was angry. Nelly was in the high chair, crying, and she wouldn't eat. Ika was standing beside her, and every time Nelly opened her mouth to cry louder, she stuffed in a bite of cheese sandwich. Nelly didn't want it, but Father said she had to have it. The plate had to be empty. And because Ika was nearly five years old, and therefore a big girl, it was up to her to feed her little sister.

Mother had said this before she'd left to go to the hospital, where Grandmother lay very sick. So sick that Ika thought she would die. Grandmother had never been one to talk much, but now she wasn't saying anything at all and all the time her eyes were closed. Grandfather hadn't wanted her to go to hospital, but the doctor had insisted on it. Because Grandfather didn't visit her, Mother had to. This much Ika had understood from the conversations between her mother and father.

Father wasn't nice when it came to Grandfather. Mother got mad, then went anyway saying, "You'll still be here. You can just as well eat with them and then put them to bed. Or is that asking too much?"

"I don't like my wife going out alone at night."

Mother's eyes grew dark, and her voice never before sounded so strange as it did when she said, "You might even say that you know all too well what can happen to a woman alone in the dark!"

Ika was afraid of Mother at that moment, and then Father had turned round. Mother had pulled her into the kitchen, and Ika resisted stiffly and anxiously when Mother clasped her against herself. Why did Mother do this? She'd never done such a thing before. Was it because she was scared Grandmother might die?

"You're a big girl. Be sure Nelly eats everything on her plate, won't you. And do it quietly, so Father doesn't get cross."

Ika nodded. She would have agreed to anything if only Mother would be like her normal self again. She then struggled free and purposefully went about setting the table so Mother would see she was looking after everything well. Yes, she could do it all very well.

While Ika was buttering the bread for sandwiches, Mother left. But when she started to spread the jam, Nelly's favorite, Father walked into the kitchen and said they were to have cheese sandwiches instead. He got the cheese out of the pantry and pared off some thin slices.

But Nelly didn't want cheese. So she threw her plate from the high chair, and it broke into smithereens on the floor. This is when Father got angry. He clenched his teeth, and his face turned red. In two steps he was standing over the high chair about to give Nelly a slap. Ika knew how hard Father could hit. He mustn't do that to Nelly. Although Ika was still very small, she jumped between the two of them and hung on to his arm to try to hold him back.

But he shook Ika off, then shifted his wrath toward her. He hit her so hard that she was thrown against the hall door, causing it to fly open with a loud bang. She fell into the hallway and slid across the granite floor as far as the hallstand. Ika jumped up in a panic and raced toward the stairs, scared all the while that he'd come after her. Instead, Father slammed the stairway door after her and turned the key.

At the top of the stairs, Ika heard the metallic noise of the key moving in the lock. And because she was more scared of being locked up than she was of Father, she spun around and ran down to the door and hit it with her fists, shouting and begging for him to open it. Finally she gave up. As she headed up to her room, halfway up the stairs her foot slipped on a step and she fell and fell and kept on falling.

Ika didn't scream, nor did she feel it when her head hit the hard granite floor at the bottom of the stairs. When she began to drift back from out of the deep waters of nothingness, there was only the cold and the pain and the taste of blood in her mouth.

Later, much later, for a long time, the curtains were closed, the bed had no pillows, and her head was full of violence.

And Grandmother was dead and buried.

As Ika bathed her eyes under the kitchen tap, she realized much had been said after all. Mother had said she should stay, and that she must know about her past. Did that mean Mother had hoped and prayed for Ika to come see her? Perhaps Mother was more afraid of her than the other way around. The cold water felt good on Ika's puffy eyelids. But the pressure behind her eyes wasn't a good sign. She sighed.

It was still only half past ten in the morning. She could expect Nelly anytime now.

## CHAPTER EIGHT

FROM WHERE SHE STOOD in front of the kitchen window, Ika saw Nelly coming. She pushed her bike in front of her through the deep gravel, looking militant. Ika prepared herself to avoid any strife, but when Nelly stepped into the kitchen, her eyes were full of tears. Ika instantly felt as if she were on shaky footing. They shook hands. In this way they had drawn closer to each other. Then came a sort of embrace, though it was the kind of embrace that above all showed their shyness, as though they were trying to sense where it would lead.

Nelly hid her emotions in what appeared to be a frantic busyness. Ika quickly picked this up. In no time at all the dishes were washed, the washing machine was droning away, and fresh coffee was brewed. Thick slices of *snijkoek*, or slab cake, were buttered and set out on a plate, for Ika would probably be hungry. She must have left early that morning. Yes, Willem had told her.

Ika watched Nelly and had to smile. Willem's approach probably worked better than the spoiling that Nelly had previously been accustomed to. Nelly had become quite the busy housewife.

Ika fed her cake to the dove, and Nelly, with red blotches on her neck, began with the question, "You got my letter then?"

A nod was enough.

"I'm glad you've come. Since Friday Mother has been so restless. She constantly talks about you. That she'd seen you."

"That would be right," Ika said quietly.

A defensive look came into Nelly's eyes as if she didn't trust the whole business. "I was here the whole day."

Ika smiled and tapped Nelly's hand, so that she wouldn't sound too reproachful. "You went around to your neighbor's for the sewing machine, and that is when I popped into Mother's corner."

Nelly's eyes grew big as she pulled her hand away.

"I came along when the mobile shop stopped here, just in front of the house, and when you were inside I walked around the back."

"But I looked in on Mother *before* I went to the neighbor's. Then later I was here again." Nelly's voice rose in surprise.

"I was sitting on the chair beside the sliding doors. You looked through the crack at Mother, but you didn't see me."

"Why didn't you say something?"

Ika shrugged. "I don't know. I didn't exactly know what I should do."

Tears streamed forth from Nelly's eyes. "And what about now?"

"I believe I have to be here," Ika said, choosing her words carefully. She was searching in amazement for that compulsion to flee, the one she'd had when still with Mother, but which she didn't have with Nelly at the table, where the sun shone on the plush velvet.

It was quiet for a long time. Ika knew Nelly was looking at her, but she didn't dare raise her eyes.

"It was so strange when you left so suddenly... then ... so unbelievable . . . and it is just as unbelievable that you're now sitting here at the table again . . ." Nelly's voice ventured.

Ika was able to nod to Nelly's words.

❦

Leaving Nelly had been the hardest part.

Everything was arranged down to the finest detail. The preparations had taken months, so nothing could go wrong. Shortly after the fight over her job at the florist's shop—the fight in which Ika finally defeated Father—she had opened her own bank account in which to deposit her salary. Mother had signed the papers before Father could prevent it. Soon Ika had found a room in the town center near the shop.

It was small, yet included a table, two chairs, and a bed. At the time she moved her things in she didn't have any possessions to speak of. But she got into the habit of bringing something with her from home each time she visited her rented room—those things that fit into her bag—such as clothes, a towel, a plate, or a cherished book.

During the lunch hour, when the shop was closed, Ika would bring her things to the rented room that was waiting for her—when the time was ripe. She knew the time to leave home would come, but she didn't know precisely when. Ika didn't doubt that her mother suspected her plans to leave. Why else did she look at her every morning as Ika made her way to the bus stop? Ika felt her mother's eyes on her back, but to turn around would have meant giving herself away.

The time came of its own accord, when everything got to the point of being unbearable. It was when Ika was sick and shaking with rage, so much so that she had wanted to slam the hall door off its mountings. Yet, with extreme self-control, she closed it quietly. At that moment she knew it was to be her last night there.

In the dark, Ika had stood at the window of her little room, seeing nothing. Only the hazy spot where her breath grew bigger and bigger.

What should she do about Nelly? She would be anxious. How would Nelly go on without her? She couldn't just leave without saying good-bye to Nelly, but she also couldn't tell Nelly. Nelly cried so easily, and what if Father was to hear?

Ika didn't sleep that night. Instead, she sat on her bed and waited until dawn. In her thoughts she had said farewell to Nelly a hundred times. Pale and apparently unmoved, she ate her last breakfast at home and then, a little bit later, she left the house.

For the last time Ika glanced at the clock, thinking it was now time to go. One look at Mother, who was buttering Nelly's bread. When she said good-bye, no sound came out of her throat. Mother looked at her, with the knife and the butter and everything in her hands.

While standing at the bus stop, she hoped Nelly would ride her bike past her before the bus arrived. If only Nelly rode by rather than stopping at the corner to wait for her friends, then she'd still be able to say something. So Ika had stood praying at the curb for Nelly, for just one moment with her. But the bus came, and Ika had to get on it. From one of the bus's windows, she waved to Nelly, who was standing holding onto her bike near the street corner. There she was, laughing with someone else, not suspecting a thing. This had been the worst thing of all. Nelly hadn't looked up once. Nelly knew nothing about the night before, nor did she realize that come that evening, Ika wouldn't be there—that she'd be gone.

Then a pain started up inside Ika that felt like something tearing. A pain that reminded her of the tearing up of cellophane paper, the kind in which the nicest bouquets in the shop were packed. She was like a loose sheet of cellophane now, cut off from the roll. The whole day as she worked, Ika couldn't stand that noise. And the road to her small room, which was only two blocks from the shop, seemed much longer than the bus ride back home.

"Do you still remember the day I left?"

"Father raised the roof," Nelly said. "He was going to fetch you back and, if necessary, get the police to bring you home. But Mother wouldn't allow it, for she knew about everything."

"Did she say that?"

Nelly nodded, and Ika just shook her head.

"After Father's getting all upset and shouting, there was silence for two weeks," Nelly went on. "Yeah, two whole weeks. It was terrible."

Ika shut her eyes. She wanted to say, "If only I'd known," but said nothing instead. For even if Ika had known, she couldn't have done anything else.

But Nelly had endured two weeks of such icy coldness all on her own. Two weeks of hateful silence. Two weeks of walking past one another and not acknowledging the other's presence. Even the prayers at the dinner table were threateningly silent, in a way that made inroads into one's very being, that made one sick, and rustled in the ears. Icy coldness—deathly quiet icy coldness.

It had been Mother's weapon, which Father had also learned to manipulate. Silence. It was the crudest weapon. The weapon of bend or break.

Ika didn't know why they had quarreled this time. She looked for a cause in herself, but couldn't find one. Maybe this time the silence wasn't about her. But she thought this was unlikely. Why was it never about Nelly?

The quarrel occurred shortly after the death of Grandmother. Mother would often go over to Grandfather's in the afternoons. So after school Ika's job was to look after Nelly. It was a good thing watching her sister wasn't very hard, because Ika suffered with recurring headaches after the concussion. She wasn't allowed to play any wild games, but whom would she play with anyhow?

Nelly would still be asleep when Ika got home. This was the nicest part, waking up Nelly. Ika would run upstairs to the little sectioned-off corner of the attic where Nelly's cot stood, and then she'd stop for a moment and look at Nelly, captivated by the peaceful rhythm of her breathing. Nelly would be lying there sleeping with her thumb in her mouth, with her blond ringlets tousled around her head.

This time always gave Ika a happy feeling. This was her sister, this beautiful little girl who slowly began to sleep more and more lightly. The thumb would fall out of her mouth. She would rub her eyes with her chubby little hands, but the eyelids would stay closed.

Then Ika would begin the song. Very softly she would sing the song from Miss Toms's kindergarten class: "The sun has got his hat on, hip hip hooray. The sun has got his hat on, and he's coming out to play." Nelly's eyes would then open and she'd reach out her little hands to Ika. It was as if Ika were a mother and Nelly her child.

So Ika didn't mind if Mother had to go see Grandfather. But Ika had noticed that Father minded very much. Even then she had already realized that, although Father and Grandfather were nice to each other, they still didn't like each other much.

On the day the silence began, Father and Mother came home from Grandfather's together. Father in front and Mother a few paces behind. Mother's face was red from crying. But her eyes weren't sad looking, just very angry.

Ika didn't dare ask what was the matter. She figured it had something to do with Grandfather, which was threatening enough. She'd be better off not knowing.

When the silence lasted and lasted, so that her tummy pain started up whenever she saw Father coming in the distance, Ika went to Aaltje, because she never needed to ask Aaltje anything. Aaltje told you of her own accord.

"Are you still going to live with your other grandpa?" Aaltje asked.

Ika felt like someone had slapped her in the face. "With who?"

Aaltje wiped her hands on the tea towel. She didn't look at Ika. "With your mother's father. He's all on his own now, since his wife has died."

Ika stood motionless and wide-eyed. "Are we going to live with Grandfather?"

"I wouldn't know," Aaltje said. "I thought I'd heard that, but I'm sure it must be wrong."

Even though Aaltje hadn't yet poured out her beaker of milk, Ika couldn't stay any longer. She had to go straight home.

But when she got home she didn't dare break the silence. Ika couldn't get the question out of her mouth. It was stupid. If Father and Mother were not talking, Ika was less and less able to say anything. The silence seemed to hollow her out. She grew so empty and cold from the oppressive quiet that every question froze on her lips.

Only her eyes still worked and they saw much more than normal. Such as Mother's face when she returned home from Grandfather's, her mouth which had become a tight fold, her hands which she always clasped in her lap, and the movement of her chest as she sighed. Ika saw Father sitting at the table, big and dominating and with piercing eyes, who made a deafening noise with his spoon, scraping at his porridge bowl. Or was this only because nobody was saying anything? Father, who appeared to be twice as big if he tilted his chair back, stood up and stretched.

To live with Grandfather! This was the worst thing Ika could imagine. It was perhaps the only time she hoped Father would win. Because if they had to go and live with Grandfather, then she'd die, just like Grandmother. That she knew for sure.

And Nelly kept babbling on in her toddler's talk throughout all the silence. She still climbed into her father's lap and hung on to his pant legs. She still played *Round and round the garden, like a teddy bear* on Mother's neck. Nobody laughed but Nelly.

But it didn't go through; they didn't go to live with Grandfather. Father had been the first to say something, to Nelly that she should eat up. Even these words had been welcome.

❦

"Who spoke first?" Ika asked Nelly.

"What do you mean?"

A smile came to Ika's lips, which contradicted the somber look in her eyes. "Whoever spoke first again had won. Did you not know that?"

Nelly looked at her dumbfounded. "I'd never noticed that, but now that you say it, you're right. But I don't know who spoke first. It ended when Mr. Molenaar came by."

Ika was completely shocked by this. "Mr. Molenaar, here? When I was away?"

Nelly's eyes narrowed in amazement. "We thought that you had sent him with a message. Did you not ask him to. . . ?"

Ika shook her head. She laid her hands palms up on the table, as if she was trying to say, "I don't know anything, honestly."

"Mr. Molenaar came here to tell us that you had a room and that you were doing your very best at the florist's shop, that they were pleased with you. And yes, now I remember, it was Mother who spoke first."

What did she say? Ika wanted to ask, but she only cleared her throat.

"She said, 'I wouldn't have expected anything else,' and then she stood up and walked out of the room, as if she didn't want to listen to Mr. Molenaar anymore. I can still remember that Father let him out. That was most unusual that Father should open the door for anyone. He looked really relieved."

Ika made a sudden movement with her head. "Relieved! Surely you don't believe he was worried about me? But Mother, how was Mother afterward?"

Nelly pondered the question for a while, then replied, "I don't know. I don't remember much after that. She was often sick, or pretended to be. Then I had to do all the things you always had been responsible for. And I didn't think that was so nice." She continued with a quick look at Ika. "I certainly know that when I was small I was spoiled rotten. But I can't do anything about that. That was the way it was here, that was the situation."

"You're right, Nelly. That was the situation. You were the only one here at home that could be loved. I was as bad as the others."

Nelly reached over the table to Ika. Her voice sounded hoarse. "But despite all that spoiling, I still didn't have a happy childhood, you know . . . just in case you ever think I had."

Ika's eyes softened. "I'll not argue with you about that, Nelly. I suppose it doesn't make much difference whether people fought against you or about you."

A sound in the front room brought them back to the present

again—to Mother, who was lying there.

"Dr. Spaan is coming this morning," Nelly said, getting up to look through the chink in the sliding doors. "Then you can hear it for yourself."

Ika stayed in the back room and heard how Nelly was speaking to Mother. She blanked out the words and just listened to the sound. Mother's voice was soft and a little raspy, but the voice was still domineering. Nelly's voice sounded high and clear, persuasive, and reassuring. Ika then realized that Nelly had taken on a lot since Mother had become seriously ill.

"Mother wants you," Nelly said as she stepped out of the front room, carrying the coffee cups and a dirty glass.

Ika stood planted by the table, her hands flat on the plush velvet. Nelly had walked through to the kitchen and left the sliding doors open. But Ika waited.

She stared at the row of photographs on the wall above the dresser. One of Father, one of Grandfather, and one of Machteld—a friend of Mother's who had died young. Machteld had hung there as long as she could remember. Both Father and Mother used to stand there looking at the photo for a long time. But when Ika asked questions about Machteld, she never got an answer. The photo of Father was taken a short time before he died. She'd never seen him so bald. The eyes looked back at her intently. There was something haughty about his face, something aloof. It was the photo of a man who could be silent for weeks on end.

Her hands were pressed beside each other on the tablecloth. She finally raised them, and a shiver ran down her spine.

Ika then peered out the nearby window to the garden where Nelly was hanging out the washing. Nelly's skirt was flapping around her legs, and the sheets clung to her body as she tried to pin them to the line. It was a good drying day.

Her attention shifted from the garden to the front room. Only the foot of Mother's bed was visible. The outline of Mother's feet under the covers was narrow and straight. The stillness of the front room called to her.

Or was it Mother's voice? But Ika walked past the open sliding doors, outside to where Nelly was hanging the last of the washing with a clothespin between her lips. Just the way Mother used to.

## CHAPTER NINE

HER LITTLE GARDEN was still there. It looked smaller now, but Ika still recognized the leaves of the yellow *Doronicum*. And the bleeding hearts still bloomed. She saw that someone had been cutting it back often enough, so the plant kept on producing new shoots.

It wasn't a picture that suited Mother, who never gathered anything other than vegetables from the garden. As Nelly shook out the last towel, she saw Ika looking. Nelly shouted that it was Abe who looked after the garden now.

Surprised, Ika asked, "And who is Abe?"

Nelly's face lit up with a laugh. She was still the child with the little kitten face when she laughed. "Abe is our eldest. He's nine and just as mad about gardening as you were."

How could that be? Abe, Nelly's child, looking after the garden here, looking after her bleeding hearts. It was Abe who was thinning out and potting things, who, with his boy's hands, was turning over the same ground, her ground.

Feeling light-headed, Ika leaned against the shed. The sun shud-

dered in the air, and the house slid away sideways, then back again.
She laughed. There was an Abe. He was nine and he liked gardening. And she didn't know this!

What did it matter that he was Nelly's son? He was her nephew.
He had her love of the black earth and the green leaf.

In a few steps she was at the back door, where Nelly was throwing the warm washing water over the path to kill the moss. It
steamed up from the tiles and tried to find a way between the
cracks. Ika didn't jump aside. She took Nelly's arm, not realizing
how different her face looked, and asked, "When can I see him?
Does he often come to see Mother?"

"Who? Abe?"

Ika nodded eagerly.

Nelly looked down at the wet path. "I hope he stays away. If he
sees that I'm dumping soapsuds all over his lovely moss, he'll go
wild."

Again a quiver shot through Ika. She walked over to the garden
and then stood for a long time by the fence. There was an Abe, her
nephew, who liked mosses and was mad about growing things. One
of her kind.

Ika visited the nursery quite often, to see Bart and his seedlings
and his flowerpots. She enjoyed the rich smell of soil in the green-

houses; she liked the broody warmth that was there. She would have liked to live there. The relationship between Bart and his father had piqued her curiosity—how the two of them treated each other like adults. Their way of talking seemed to have nothing to do with their being father and son. This was unimaginable to Ika.

Bart would bike across the village and greet her as he rode past by throwing his head backward. It got to the point where Ika thought every blond boy was Bart.

Even so, they once had a terrible fight, so bad that Ika didn't care to visit the nursery again. She didn't return even when her bleeding hearts had so many seedlings, or when the *Doronicum* was nearly eaten away by slugs. It had been a strange quarrel that concerned Bart's mother and her mother.

"I'm never going to marry! I'll always stay with my father," Bart had said.

"Why?" Ika asked, perplexed.

Bart flattened a little mound of soil with his foot. His eyes were dark. "Because women are mean, and men aren't."

Ika had shaken her head. "Well, what makes you think such a thing?"

"They're never satisfied and end up going their own way. My father said so himself." Then Bart's face had grown deep red, and Ika thought he was going to cry. "When you need 'em, they're never there," he screamed.

Bart wasn't acting like his usual self. Ika had become scared and so walked toward the door. She thought she'd better get away. With her hand on the shed's door, she hesitated and then said, "But not with us, you know. My mother is always there."

Bart gave a kick at a flowerpot that was lying at his feet. A shard broke off and flew sideways through a pane of glass, which fell tinkling down. A fright ran through Ika.

All at once everything seemed much worse than just the broken pot and the tinkling glass. She pushed with all her might, but the heavy door only yielded a little.

"Your mother's a wicked hag too," Ika heard Bart calling from behind, while she ran as hard as she could along the slippery path between the greenhouses. She reached the road panting and began to walk slowly now because of the cramp in her side. Pressing her hand against her side helped. She kept turning around, but saw that Bart wasn't following her. He had called her mother a bad name, and it wasn't true.

A few days later, as Ika was sitting quietly at the table, Mother and the neighbor were in the front room sipping coffee and talking.

"Did you know that the woman from the nursery on Heren Street has gone off again? Well, you know, it hasn't been going well for a while. It was never right. Yeah, somebody else, what would you think? That hadn't been a good match for a long time. At least there's only one child. He's at the public school. Must be about eleven. No, they haven't been to church for ages now, not since they got married. It's Reformed I would imagine, if it suited them at Christmas."

Ika knew they were talking about Bart's mother, and about

Bart, who hadn't a mother any longer.

Ika stood up to peek through the sliding doors and looked at her mother's intently listening face. The sun was shining directly on her hair, and it looked as if she were wearing a golden crown. "Wicked hag," Bart had said. But that didn't apply to her mother. Certainly not.

"Why did you not come?" Mother asked, when Ika finally stepped in through the sliding doors into the front room.

"Nelly was with you and she can help you better than I can." Immediately Ika rebuked herself for having said the last part of that sentence. It wasn't necessary to invent excuses. She was here for Mother, but she could only do this if Mother allowed her the space to be herself. This whole thing was already hard enough. She wasn't like Mother and she didn't want to be. Surely if she'd been like Mother, she probably wouldn't have been standing there.

Ika focused on Mother's eyes. Blue gray and bloodshot. Eyes that seemed always to put up a struggle. "I can't go along with this, Mother. I'll stay as long as I want to. I came here on my conditions, not yours."

Mother's expression grew even more grim and painful looking. "I'm sick, Ikabod, and I have little time left. Did you come for the dove or the garden, then?"

*There is no sense in trying to appease her, to play it down*, Ika told herself. *I won't be set on Mother's track—for her to tell me the direction and way. This is what I want. I want to be with her, but in my way. I want her to see me as a person and not as the child that should never have been.*

By the way Mother's eyelids flickered, Ika could tell she was slowly getting angry. Her mouth became a thin line.

"Did you come for the dove or the garden?" she repeated.

Ika thought about the dove that had recognized her, and of the boy's hands that had been working in her garden. "In a certain sense, yes," she answered.

It seemed as if Mother wanted to say something, but then she turned her face toward the wall.

A strange relief came over Ika and with it the feeling that the roles had been reversed. She closed the sliding doors behind her and went to look for Nelly who was peeling potatoes in the kitchen. Ika sat down at the little kitchen table and listened to the potatoes as they plopped into the water.

"I'm staying here, Nelly. I'll stay as long as it takes."

Nelly stopped her peeling. Then, openmouthed, she turned and stared at Ika.

Dr. Spaan came in the afternoon. Ika saw the old black sedan pull up in front of the house. Nelly hurried to the front door to let him in. Soon Ika could hear the droning sound of his voice coming from the hall. Through the partly open door, the doctor caught sight of Ika, and his eyebrows disappeared under the brim of his hat. He was so much the same as he had always been that Ika felt herself grow smaller. Her name danced in the front of her mind in letters of fire. She was sure that the first word Dr. Spaan would say would be her name.

He crossed the room in two paces. She had to look up at him. A large hand was held out to her and, hesitantly, she took it. "Ikabod! I knew I'd meet you here today or tomorrow. How do you find your mother?"

Ika gave a half smile and wrested her hand free. "She's sick, but beyond that still the same as ever, Doctor."

With an astonished look on her face, Nelly glanced over at Ika.

Dr. Spaan removed his hat, which suddenly made him appear much older and grayer. "Just so. She keeps up appearances, that is her way. But I assume you're not taken in."

Ika wished he would stop looking at her and stop talking. She wanted to go outside to her garden or take a walk in the meadow a short distance away. But she couldn't get past Dr. Spaan. He had barred the way, both literally and figuratively, with his finger nearly stabbing her chest.

"Now then, are you taken in or not?" he asked.

Reluctantly Ika said, "I don't know what you mean, Doctor, but I'll get to the bottom of it."

A quick smile flashed across his face. "Lovely. So you're staying here at the house?"

When Ika had nodded, the doctor walked over and threw open the sliding doors.

Mother sat on her bed, held upright by the pillows. Red blotches from the fever marked her sunken cheeks. "You're late," she snapped.

"Is that so?" Dr. Spaan retorted as he tossed his coat over the arm of a nearby chair.

Ika turned and ran outside to see if the washing was dry yet. What was it about Mother that irritated her so much? Was it her high and mighty attitude? Was it her bossiness?

"You're not going back there!" Mother demanded, just as Ika was trying to decide whether or not she should go and see Bart one more time. As if Mother had read her mind.

"Why not?"

"Because I don't want you to."

Ika wished to know why Mother would say this, but Mother's eyes prevented her. It would be better to hold her tongue. She'd go to Aaltje or Grandpa instead. Mother nodded that her going over to Grandpa's was allowed. Yet, as Ika was pulling on her boots in the kitchen doorway, she could feel Mother's gaze on her back. Ika looked up.

"I'll ask them, you know. I'll ask how long you were there."

Did Mother think she went secretly to the nursery, just because it was on the way? Indignantly she looked into Mother's stern face. "I have never lied to you."

"Let's keep it that way" was Mother's reply.

While walking toward the farm, Ika wondered why Mother was so much different toward her than she was toward Nelly. Was it because she was bigger, or because Nelly was less naughty? Maybe because Nelly was more cheerful. She was always laughing or singing.

Ika would love to have been cheerful, but she didn't know how to go about it. Cheerfulness had to begin inside. The same with laughter. Like being afraid, which also started inside a person. As she walked on, Ika made her boots squeak by dragging them through the tall, wet grass. So how could she become cheerful? Bart said that being afraid evoked the threat of danger. Would thinking more about happiness, then, help her to experience what it was like to be cheerful?

She began to list all the things that made her happy. There were a surprising number of them: the trees, the birds, the flowers, the dove, Mother and the sunlight on her hair, Nelly when she was waking up, Aaltje, Mr. Molenaar, the *Doronicum* and the *Dicentra* . . .

Then her thoughts turned to Bart, who had said he would think up a Dutch name for Ikabod. But would he still keep his promise now that they had had a fight? Bart hadn't really been angry with her, but with his mother. And she hadn't been angry either, only scared.

Would she be able to visit him again after a while, or was her seeing him forbidden for good? She decided to try to be sweet and cheerful, so that Mother would notice how she was doing her very best.

After she had drunk her milk with Aaltje, Ika helped Grandpa clean out the milk churns. Aaltje couldn't scrub that day because of her chapped hands. It was a lot of work, scrubbing like that. Ika got very warm doing it. And Grandpa was spitting the juice from his wad of tobacco close behind her in the grass, which made her shudder. Mostly because of the brown streak at the corner of his mouth. But Ika decided to sing about the owl that was sitting in the elm tree. She would try harder to be a thoughtful and happy girl and to not be so scared anymore.

"Well now," said Grandpa, "you're going a bit over the top there!"

Ika grazed her hand on the rough edge of a lid and then came the wave of heat behind her eyes.

Nelly had the ironing board out, ready to start the pressing now that Dr. Spaan had left. The smell of the wind-dried sheets was a smell from the past. Ika ironed as if she'd never ironed before. It gave her the feeling of doing something for Mother and still being out of harm's way. *Things haven't changed much*, Ika thought.

Ika decided to begin thinking about the winter garden. It seemed as though Simone and Berger's Landscape Gardening had moved to another planet. But her thoughts of the proposed garden soon became jumbled with images of Mother, Nelly, and what the future might hold.

She had just put away the ironing board when someone knocked on the front door. Nelly opened it and steered the visitor through the sliding doors. Something about the darkly dressed woman was familiar to Ika, yet she couldn't put a name to her.

Nelly came into the kitchen to put on the kettle for tea. "Mrs. Verhagen. Looks like she's here for a bit."

"From the shoe shop?" Ika asked.

Nelly nodded. "Her husband's dead. She runs the business now with Jantien. You know who I mean. Jantien, with the glasses."

Ika still remembered. Jantien used to be teased just like her. The lenses in her glasses were so strong they made her eyes look like the eyes of a surprised cow, and a lot of children found that very funny. "Is Jantien not married?"

Nelly shook her head at the same time as setting teacups on a tray. "She's got contact lenses now," Nelly went on, without her asking. "She looks an awful lot better now. Still, she's getting on toward thirty-five."

Nelly certainly didn't mean anything by it, as she said it so innocently. But the words touched a sore spot in Ika. Nelly may as well have shouted that a person couldn't outgrow her childhood years just like that. And so the old proverb still held true: *You are what you are, and you can never change that.* Ika wondered if Nelly wasn't also talking about her.

Maybe she should look Jantien up some time. But Ika put this thought out of her mind right away. What had she in common with Jantien? This village mustn't suck her in again. She was here because she had to be, for Mother and for Nelly. As soon as she could, she'd return again to the life she had built for herself. Yes, when she had drawn a line under everything here, then she'd leave. Maybe sometime she would ask about Abe paying her a visit—that is, if the winter garden turned out the way she envisioned it. Later, when things were ordinary and quiet again.

## CHAPTER TEN

WITH A PROCESSION of dark clouds scudding across the horizon, evening fell. Exactly where the sun was setting, a short but fierce burst of flame raged in the dark gray sky, and Ika stood looking at it from the back window. She missed being able to look out as far as the horizon.

Nelly had gone home. She was now alone with Mother, and the two of them had hardly exchanged a word. The threshold into the front room seemed to be getting higher and higher. Ika had sat for an hour at the drawing board, but no ideas occurred to her regarding the design for the winter garden. She knew she'd have to be patient and wait for something to come. This wasn't the kind of task a person picks up at will. The idea first had to be born, then she could begin to play around with it, try different arrangements, and work on giving it shape.

The sudden braking of a bicycle caused Ika to look out at the road. The high hedge shook violently as if someone had thrown something against it, probably the bike. Then there was the sound of gravel crunching, coupled by the image of a crew-cut head gliding past the window. Ika caught a glimpse of brown eyes and a face full of freckles. *That must be Abe*, she thought. *And it looks like he's brought chicken-noodle soup.*

The sight of him waiting outside the kitchen door had caused a lump to form in Ika's throat. He stood there looking at the pan in his hands. Some of the noodles had escaped and were now sticking to the pan's lid. When Ika swung the door open, Abe took a quick step backward. He looked from the pan to her and then back to the pan again. With a slow and guilty gesture, he raised his shoulders and stuck the pan out toward Ika.

"The stringy bits have come out," Abe confessed.

As Ika went to take the saucepan from him she didn't notice the greasy handles. So when Abe let go, the pan slipped from her hands and clanked with its heavy bottom onto the gravel path. The lid had shot off, resulting in the soup sloshing over the rim.

"Oh no! Now there'll be no more noodles at all," Abe said, looking shocked.

A feeling somewhere between laughing and crying swept over Ika. Laughing won out. Abandoning herself to it, she sank down in the doorway. Abe wiped his hands on his pants, and then a broad grin spread across his face. His smile reminded Ika of Willem. "There's still enough noodles," she said, pulling herself up on the doorjamb. "Now come and wash your hands."

Abe stepped over the saucepan and spilled soup and went into the kitchen, while Ika picked up the pan and followed him in. She watched how he washed then drank from the splashing stream of water, how he dried his hands on the blue-checkered hand towel.

"Have you really got enough?" he asked.

Ika leaned against the kitchen counter and nodded reassuringly. "How did you manage carrying that pan on your bike? Under the carrier straps?"

"Yeah. Mum said I should walk, but my bike was standing outside, and everything was going fine until I got to the ramp at the end of the street. Then, just for a second, I forgot about the soup."

He had said "Mum"—as in Nelly. It appeared inexplicable to Ika that this boy had been born to Nelly and Willem. Abe stood there with the towel still in his hand as if he were hers. Warmed by the thought, she said, "So you must be Abe."

"And you're Auntie Ika."

Then they both had to laugh.

"How many kids do you want when you're grown up?" Nelly asked Ika. The two girls were at Grandpa's out in the cowshed. Both had brought along a doll. Ika's doll was allowed in Nelly's tiny baby carriage, to sit beside Nelly's. Ika had to think about the question for a bit. Nelly had already said she wanted four, then went about stacking up bales of hay, struggling to make a house for them and their dolls.

When Ika's answer finally came, Nelly had forgotten all about her question.

"I would like one from a faraway country," Ika said, "who hasn't got a mother anymore, one that's very sad or sick. A baby boy that nobody wants. Then I'll look after him properly and make him happy and well again." After a moment of thinking about what she'd said, Ika continued, "I won't have a father, because I don't want one. Yes, no father."

Nelly thought not having a father was stupid. For if a child had no father, then the mother would always have to be at home to look after the children and wouldn't be able to attend the Women's Club meetings in the village.

"Well," Ika said angrily, "look at us now. We have a father, but does he ever look after us? And can Mother ever get out to the Women's Club?"

"No," said Nelly, "but you've got to arrange that beforehand—before you get married."

Ika had stood there dumbfounded, staring at her. How had Nelly come by such wisdom?

❧

"Can I still go in and see Granny?" Abe asked as he walked into the room.

Ika nodded. His granny was her mother. Ika could hardly believe this either.

Abe was clearly at home here. Walking past the dove, he reached up as far as he could to tap on the cage. The dove immediately cooed, and Abe imitated its call to a tee.

Mother had heard from the front room that Abe was there. She called him, and her voice sounded different. Ika followed him and then watched from between the sliding doors how he greeted Mother. He pushed up beside her on the bed and took her hand. His voice was confidential.

Mother's eyes. Why did those eyes hurt her so much? As if she would begrudge this to Abe.

Ika walked slowly back to the kitchen and to the pan of chicken-noodle soup. She cleaned up the outside of the pan and put it on the stove, setting the burner to low. Deciding she couldn't return to the front room again, Ika waited in the kitchen till Abe came out. A grandmother and her eldest grandchild—logical, and a good thing they got on so well together.

Mother's eyes. And Abe had taken her hand and made his voice go all quiet. She ought to ask him about the garden, and whether the *Doronicum* had bloomed this spring.

Ika turned up the heat on the burner. *Maybe Abe wanted to stay and have a bowl of soup*, she thought. Pulling out a wooden spoon from the drawer by the stove, Ika began to stir the soup with a methodical motion. Even though she was staring at the swirling liquid and noodles, all she could see was Mother's eyes and how they looked at Abe.

The strong smell of burning potatoes brought her back to her senses. Ika quickly filled up the pan with water, potatoes and all. She still wasn't hungry. A little of Mother's soup would be enough. Then the door opened, and Abe sniffed the smell of the potatoes.

"Aha!" he said.

Ika couldn't get herself to ask Abe if he wanted to stay and have some soup. She watched silently as he zipped up his jacket.

"Well, I'll be going," he said. "We eat at six o'clock."

Ika nodded and held the kitchen door open for him.

"Bye," he said, running down the path. She saw his shadow pass the window and noticed how the hedge moved again when he retrieved his bike. He was whistling. Soon the little song disappeared.

Ika turned off the burner and sat down at the kitchen table. In a sudden bout of anxiety, she had the feeling she'd never stand again. Life would always go on without her.

She was standing on the side, looking on. Abe, a boy like Abe. She laid her head on her folded arms. Even the varnish on the kitchen table smelled of the past. It would just have to get dark and cold.

Night. Sleep. Not to go to Mother anymore with soup. Not to talk anymore, or to see the red spots on Mother's back. No more using the hair-dryer.

But the dove kept calling with an insistent cooing. It tugged at her. It questioned and begged her. With leaden legs, Ika stood up. The kitchen had already become dusky, and when she walked into the living room, the darkness had nestled in the corners and in the velvet curtains. She switched on the floor lamp.

The dove was asleep, its head tucked into its feathers. Then Mother called. With dull reluctance, Ika pushed open the sliding doors. There in the front room it was completely dark. Only the white of the sheets could be seen, which seemed to glow now. Her flipping on the light filled the entire room with a bright whiteness. The body in the bed was so shocked that she instantly switched it off again. So Ika found a table lamp near Mother's bed, a milder light, streaming out from a yellow-brown shade and giving off a warm homey feeling that transformed the space.

She could now go and sit on the edge of the bed, just as Abe had done. In the room's softness Mother's eyes were dark and exhibited a faint light without harshness, without questions. She took the hand that was lying on the sheet. It felt dry and cool, like parchment.

"I thought you had gone away," Mother whispered.

Ika shook her head. "I'll get you some soup," she said after a long silence.

As Ika stood up, Mother said, "I need to use the bathroom."

It was the sound of her voice, the hesitation, the "would you mind very much if. . . ?" that had made it easy for Ika. "Then we'll do that first," Ika said.

Helping her out of bed, Ika was shocked at how little Mother weighed. Mother kept her lips pressed tightly together so as not to moan, for it was difficult for Ika to hold Mother firmly without hurting her. But in spite of her clumsiness, Ika saw the incident as a victory.

Grandmother—Mother's mother—had been in a wheelchair for the final years of her life. During this time, she suffered with advanced diabetes and so had little control of her legs. For Ika, Grandmother had become more important precisely because of the wheelchair.

Grandfather didn't want to push the wheelchair. But Mother said he *couldn't* push the chair. Ika understood. She had a hard time imagining her grandfather pushing a wheelchair. The act didn't suit him: he with his black coat and hat, with his cigar. He'd never ridden a bike either. He always walked. "A bicycle is undignified," he'd once said in her presence.

Since Grandmother had been confined to the wheelchair, Ika visited the failing woman out of her own free will, as if she had always needed an excuse before. And Grandmother enjoyed Ika's visits. She didn't actually say as such, but Ika could tell. For instance, when Ika used to push the wheelchair through the gravel to the road and, panting, need to stop for a brief rest, she would often notice a change in her grandmother's face. The change was usually subtle: the blinking of her eyes, and the straight line of her mouth that went all soft. Back at the manse Grandmother's face had the look of one who was miserable and melancholy. Ika couldn't remember ever having heard her laugh. Nobody laughed in the manse. Only Nelly sometimes, but then Mother would appear shocked and tell Nelly to quiet down at once.

On many occasions Ika would push the wheelchair through the streets and over to the riverbank. Grandmother loved the river. Ika always parked the heavy chair near the edge of the bank between the rows of houses overlooking the water. Then the two of them would wait till a boat chugged by, which sometimes took a long time. But Ika didn't mind.

Grandmother talked about growing up and her father once having a boat. It was impossible for Ika to imagine her grandmother as a girl on a boat, one with pigtails and a flapping skirt. It seemed as though Grandmother had always been old, silent, and serious.

One particular afternoon, when they were at the riverbank and watching for a boat, Grandfather appeared. Ika recognized him coming from far away, for nobody walked the way he did. "Grandmother," she had said, "Grandfather's coming." Her voice sounded a bit hesitant, as if Grandfather wouldn't approve of what they were doing—waiting there by the river and looking for boats.

"I hear a boat," Grandmother had said. "Do you hear the noise of the engine in the distance?"

Ika heard very faintly the dull throb of an engine drawing nearer. Grandfather was also coming nearer. It seemed like a race between Grandfather and the boat, which gave Ika an anxious feeling. At the moment Grandfather passed them by, the prow of the boat came around the bend in the river. Grandmother pointed toward the boat, her arm shaking.

Later, as Ika was pushing the wheelchair up the ramp and through the front door of the manse, she saw that Grandfather was standing in the hall. Ika stepped around him to get a cloth from the kitchen to wipe off the chair's wheels. When she returned, Grandfather was still standing there looking at her. With a red face, Ika polished the wheels until they were sparkling clean.

Ika looked up at him and wondered if she should ask if she'd cleaned the wheelchair to his satisfaction. Suddenly Grandfather took her chin in his big white hand, and Ika felt her whole body become stiff. He stared at her long and hard. *I hope I don't start to cry*, she thought.

Then he said something Ika didn't understand: " 'For to him that is joined to all the living there is hope; for a living dog is better than a dead lion.' " For the longest time she had only remembered the "living dog" and the "dead lion" and that Grandfather's voice neither had been angry nor severe. Maybe he was glad that she'd gone with Grandmother to the river after all.

Ika warmed up the soup again and brought it in to Mother. She fluffed up the pillows behind Mother's back and then laid a napkin on her chest. Spoonful by spoonful Ika fed her the chicken-noodle soup. Ika felt a sharp pain in her lower back from sitting in the same position too long. Yet Mother was eating and, according to Nelly, that was the most important thing.

After Ika had eaten as well, Mother asked if she would read to her. Ika pulled out the small Bible from the bedside table. She looked at Mother, but Mother did not return her gaze. She lay back on her pillow with her eyes closed.

Ika leafed through to the bookmark. She struggled to get herself to read the passage. It went against her will to read the story of Eli's death, the story about her name. " 'And she named the child Ichabod, saying, The glory is departed from Israel, because the ark of God was taken, and because of her father-in-law and her husband. And she said, The glory is departed from Israel, for the ark of God is taken.' "

Her voice didn't falter, and the words had sounded quiet, clear.

There was a cold space inside her, which had helped her to read calmly. When she had closed the Bible she saw tears on Mother's cheeks that reflected the dim light of the table lamp. But because of the cold space in her chest, Ika was able to stand up and clear away the empty dishes without saying anything. Speaking in a murmur, Mother said grace. While Ika was washing the dishes, the familiar words of the prayer came back to her, and with the words came Father's face.

After finishing cleaning up the kitchen Ika found the old photo album. She sat down at the table under the bright light and looked through it carefully, turning page after page. Ika studied the photos of Mother when she was young, which showed her with a mischievous look that Ika had never seen. Photos of Mother with her friend, who had died young, standing near the water's edge in the spring. Sweet-looking faces. Photos with Mr. Molenaar. She and Nelly together on a bench. Nelly laughing and beaming, and she surly and leaning backward, as if searching for a way of escape.

She found the manse, too, with its blooming border of red salvias. Recalling that this was the first color photo she had set eyes on, Ika remembered how at the time she'd thought it was marvelous. Now the colors appeared artificial to her.

Another photo showed Father by the shed with his hand on his bike. He was laughing for the photo, but she couldn't remember having seen him laugh like that.

Grandpa's farm. Nelly with the goats. And then, surprisingly, a picture of herself, pushing the wheelchair with Grandmother in it. The photo was taken while she was pushing the wheelchair up onto the pavement on the way toward the river. It was clear to see how she was using all her weight to push the chair. Her legs were braced, with her hands and chest against the handles.

Grandmother with her eyes closed. Yes, this was how she often sat. But by the river her eyes were always open. She'd never seen this photo before. It was a mystery to her who had taken it.

Grandmother's face looked like Mother's as it was now. It had never occurred to Ika before, but now they seemed like one face. Mother lying back on the pillows and Grandmother in the wheelchair halfway onto the pavement on the way to the river.

## CHAPTER ELEVEN

THE TINY BEDROOM was located directly above the front room. Little had changed in the bedroom. The narrow bed sat close to the sloping roof. The same blue-striped curtains still hung beside the two small windows.

Ika wondered if from upstairs she'd hear Mother if she called. Willem said she would, because he had slept there on previous nights.

Ika changed the sheets and put her suitcase in the closet. She didn't unpack. She still wanted to cling to the idea that she could leave at a minute's notice.

The picture she'd received years ago as a gift from Mr. Molenaar still hung on the wall. This was when she learned to say the Ten Commandments by heart. She still remembered it. Toward the bottom of the picture was written "Suffer the little children to come unto me, and forbid them not, for of such is the kingdom of God." The verse suited the drawing well. Jesus with children from every race gathered around Him.

There had been a bit of a to-do surrounding the picture, so it was a wonder the picture was still on display. Ika brushed the dust off the frame. At the time the picture's presence had made her less anxious. It had been the opposite of Grandfather's preaching. Ika wondered who had framed it. She would ask Nelly later. She smiled as she remembered how the picture had comforted her. All Grandfather's preaching would fade into the background when she stared at Jesus and the children.

Ika was about eleven. She wasn't sleeping well. She would often sit at the window late into the evening, counting the cars that rumbled past the corner further down the street. After twenty had gone by, she could again try to sleep. But sometimes she began obsessively counting a second twenty. This took longer, of course, and then it would become really late because of there not being many cars at such an hour. Ika couldn't bear it in her bed and she didn't dare go downstairs. Father didn't like it when she went downstairs after saying good-night.

And she didn't dare pray, though praying sometimes seemed the best thing to do. When she prayed, she got the feeling that God could see her—her sin and her badness. Then she heard in her head Grandfather's sermons, about the wrath of God that couldn't tolerate sin. Also in the Bible were those terrifying stories about fire that fell from heaven, of people who dropped dead because of a lie, or about the pestilence that walked in darkness. Even though she didn't know precisely what it was, it all sounded so frightful.

And then Ika was given the picture of Jesus and the children. They were ordinary children. There at the feet of Jesus was a girl in a light blue dress and a little black boy wearing only a loincloth. Also pictured was a Chinese child and, sitting in Jesus' lap, an Indian girl wearing a tiny sari. Jesus had His arm around the shoulders of a girl with a grass skirt and a necklace of shells. He loved them all. Ika could see that. It didn't matter where the children were from or what they looked like. Ika had been so pleased with the picture, and her teacher, Mr. Molenaar, noticed her delight.

"Are you there too, Ika?" he had asked.

At first she had remained quiet, doubting that such a thing could be possible.

"I can see you there," the teacher said. "Between the Chinese child and the small black boy. I believe there's somebody else there leaning on Jesus' knee."

It wasn't true, yet when the teacher said it, Ika could see it after all. They understood each other, and Ika thought it was a pity that there were no big people among the children.

But Mr. Molenaar explained, "In the eyes of Jesus we are all children, Ika. So I'm in the picture too. Can't you see me?"

When she got home she showed the picture to Mother. Like a costly jewel, Ika had carried it home between her dress and her jacket. *As long as nobody attacks me from behind,* she thought. *As long as I don't have to run.*

But no one paid her any attention as she left the playground. It was as if Jesus himself was offering her His protection.

Mother looked over the picture, while Ika, full of expectation, looked at Mother's face. Surely Mother would like it, for it was so beautiful.

But Mother pushed the picture away and said, "It's a sin to make a picture of God, or of Jesus. You've just learned that yourself—the second commandment. And now you're coming home with a picture like this. Mr. Molenaar, I'm sure. It's a good thing Grandfather doesn't know about this!"

Ika took the picture and hid it. It wasn't till much later that she dared to hang it up, when she didn't care what Mother thought about it. And Grandfather hardly ever came to their house, and if he did, he never came upstairs.

How could Mother not have seen how Jesus was looking? How could she just push the picture away?

Ika felt scared for Mother because she couldn't find her in the picture. However much she tried, Mother wasn't there. She didn't mind so much that she couldn't find Grandfather and Father. Nelly was certainly there, and Grandmother too. So shouldn't Mother also be able to be found?

❧

Through the floorboards, Ika could hear her mother coughing. Probably she shouldn't sleep so soundly. But if Mother needed her, she would be downstairs in an instant.

She turned off the light and went downstairs.

Mother's eyes were reproachful. Ika understood. She hadn't sat much with her mother that day. Picking up an encyclopedia of garden plants, she sat down in the chair by the table lamp.

As Ika thumbed slowly through the book she could feel Mother's eyes on her.

Mother sighed every now and then. Ika began to listen to the sighing and soon got the feeling Mother was trying to vex her. She put down the book and looked at her.

Mother's hands restlessly smoothed the sheet over and over again.

"Can I do anything for you?" Ika asked softly.

"Nobody can do anything for me," was her reply. It was incredible how Mother could manage to kill off any feelings of tenderness. Could there be no ordinary conversation between them?

Ika began to talk about the winter garden. She told about the commission and the work involved with the project. Mother kept her eyes closed, but still Ika had the feeling she was listening.

When Ika had finished talking and it was quiet for a while, Mother said, "They think of everything nowadays. Who would have thought of a winter garden?"

"Well, I would have." Ika sounded proud.

"But nothing grows in the winter."

"You'd be surprised. There are plants that bloom as early as January, and a lot of shrubs are evergreen."

"Imagine earning your living doing that," Mother said with scorn in her voice.

Ika picked up the book again, though she'd lost the inclination to read. She then put up with more of Mother's drawn-out sighing.

A few moments later, Mother stated, "It's too bright in here. Can you turn off one of the table lamps?"

"It'll have to be the one by your bed, because this one's staying on," Ika said without looking up.

Mother didn't answer; she just turned her face to the wall.

Ika took paper and pen from her bag and made some notes. She began to get deep into her thoughts, seeing the contours of a semicircular glass dome form in her mind's eye, a dome with a removable section at the front that could be dismantled for the summer. The walking path would loop around from the hall along the glass wall like two arms, as if the middle were being pressed to the heart in a kind of embrace. The hall of the hotel would always act as the beating heart of the whole design. For there was located the main reception area, the bar, and the lounge.

An engine had started up within Ika. In her thoughts she began to talk over her design ideas with Simone. Would it have to be firmly fixed there under the glass wall? Definitely. Then they should take that into account. She made a note for Simone.

She was startled by Mother's voice, which had sounded bitter. "I would've thought it far better to have a husband and children.

That's what a woman is for, you know. Not what you're going after. All that digging around in the dirt. I don't know who you got that from."

Ika stood up, gathered her things, and walked to the back room. On the threshold between the sliding doors she looked around. "I don't know who I got it from either. There's a lot I don't know. I don't even know who my father was."

"You certainly didn't get this need to dig in the dirt from your father."

Ika dropped her bag. While she was bending to pick it up, she said, "Well, now at least I know something. I don't get my love of gardening from him."

At the table in the back room Ika tried to resume her work on the design, but it didn't work. All at once the idea of the embrace seemed idiotic.

Everything remained quiet in the front room. Not a good silence, but a silence full of bitterness and reproach. Ika wondered whether she should perhaps call Simone and have a chat. But Simone would ask how things were going with her mother. Then what would Ika say? No one could lie to Simone and get away with it.

With her head in her hands, Ika took stock of the day. There was Abe. That had been the best part of her day. And Nelly too. Seeing Nelly again was good. Dr. Spaan, but what had he meant by being so cryptic about Mother. Mother . . .

She'd always known what Mother would be like. Ika had no

illusions concerning her. She mustn't become sentimental. Such feelings would be no help to her.

She got up to warm some milk. Leaning against the counter, she saw herself reflected in the kitchen window. The straight hair framing her face, the line of her neck, and the drooping shoulders. *Lanky* was the word that came to mind.

Then she heard footsteps coming around the back, and with a jerk, the back door was pulled open. The gas flame under the milk spluttered with the gust of wind. Willem kicked off his shoes and creaked into the wicker chair.

"Well, I thought I'd better come and take a look to see how things are here."

Ika turned down the burner just in time to stop the milk from boiling over.

"What are you doing, making porridge?" Willem asked.

She couldn't resist laughing any longer. "Warming up some milk. Would you like some too?"

He turned up his nose and, with a quick movement of his head toward the front room, asked, "How's everything going?"

Ika shrugged her shoulders. "I don't know. She's in pain, I think."

"She's feeling awkward," Willem said sympathetically. "That's nice."

He struggled getting out of the chair. After finally attaining a standing position, he lumbered over to the front room. Ika followed with the two beakers of warm milk. With a jerk, Willem pushed the sliding doors further open and then pulled a chair up to the bed.

Ika was surprised to see a smile creeping over Mother's face as she set down the milk. She held her breath and waited. Willem kept his voice at what was for him the usual volume, yet in the front room it sounded sacrilegious. "Well, did you run the marathon today, or have you just been lying here lazy?"

Ika couldn't believe her ears. What was it about this man that he could speak to Mother in that tone, and that she would accept it too? Was this what Dr. Spaan had meant by his "getting through to her"? Getting through the way Willem did, in his unashamed, endearing manner? Why could she not do this? Mother enjoyed it, Ika could see that.

She'd never seen Mother look at her in the way she looked at Willem. Why was everything so difficult between Mother and her? Was it because she couldn't approach Mother uninhibited? Because all the past was in the room, in their glances, in their words? Willem talked randomly about one thing and then another, bits of news in the village, about the boys, about his work. A skin grew on the milk, but Ika didn't bother with it as she was listening just like Mother.

Willem put in the edging that runs along ditches and lakes. It was heavy work, but just the thing for someone as restless as he was, as he said himself. In the open air and always moving around to new places. Better than sitting behind a desk.

"Do you do ponds as well?" Ika heard herself asking.

"Only large ones that need a firm edge. For a smaller pond, you'd do better to go to a garden center."

❧

There had been an advertisement in the paper: "Summer workers needed at garden center." Although Ika never went there anymore, she knew immediately that the ad was referring to Bart's father's business. There was only one nursery on the village's main street.

Ika had passed all her exams and so was free earlier that year. She was excited about the prospect of spending her summer working with flowers and plants. She felt it would be better to go ahead and apply rather than ask. Still, Ika decided to cut out the advertisement and leave it lying on the table for a day, to prepare Mother. This usually worked.

But then Father saw the ad and started in. "Ikabod, what was that clipping doing there on the table? What are you up to now?"

*Don't look at him*, Ika thought. *Just be normal, give him a casual reply.* If he noticed that it was important to her, then he'd be against it. "Oh . . . well, staying at home all the time, there isn't much to do. The summer holiday is coming up and I thought the job would be fun and also good preparation for the horticultural college." While talking, Ika continued to clear the table.

Father had derided the idea of her attending the horticultural college, saying it was a shame that, instead of using her brains, she wanted to dig around in the dirt. But he'd not said anything more about the summer job. Mother only looked at her.

So the next morning, with her heart pounding away, Ika went to the garden center. She hadn't been there for a long time. At first Mother had forbidden it, and later she'd been too big to go and play with a boy.

Ika recognized the tall blondish man right away—Bart's father. But he'd grown much older. His face was now covered with hundreds of fine wrinkles. Ika especially noticed his hands, which were hard and calloused and strangely familiar. And when he laughed, he reminded her of Bart.

"Weren't you a friend of my son's some time ago?"

Ika nodded, and then they chatted for a while. She ended up getting the information she desired without having to ask.

"Bart's in America for a year," the older man explained. "Work experience. So you mentioned you saw my ad. Did you come looking for a job, then? You'll have to begin work next Monday. How does that sound?"

Ika endured the heat of the greenhouses for seven long weeks. It had been a hot summer. Ever since then the damp fermenting smell of the warm soil reminded her of that summer, and also of Bart. Even though she didn't see Bart, she still got to know him a lot better. Bart's father read Bart's weekly letters to the garden center workers during coffee breaks. The letters talked a lot about his job in America. Bart's father read them in a tone that for Ika was inconceivable. How could a father talk about his child in such a manner, with so much love and pride in his voice?

❦

Ika interrupted Willem's story. "Is that garden center still there on Heren Street?"

Willem thought about it, then shook his head. "No. As far as I know, it's not there anymore. You mean Hogerveer's. That's now further up on the canal, over the railway. Do you know where I mean?"

Ika nodded. She was afraid to ask if Willem happened to know who the owner or manager was now. Maybe Bart had never come back from America.

Willem stood and stretched, his fingers nearly touching the low ceiling. "Sleep well now, and don't moan too much," he said to Mother. He then gave Ika a wink.

After Ika with trembling hands had tended Mother's back, she climbed the stairs and closed herself into her little room. She lay awake for a long time and heard Mother twisting and turning in the room below. Sometimes Ika heard her groan and murmur something. But Mother never called for her that night. How could she not need her even once? Was it that Mother didn't want her, or that she did not want to ask for her help? Ika just lay there waiting in between the times she heard Mother, when she finally nodded off and dreamed.

A little before four o'clock in the morning Ika went downstairs and tiptoed through the dark hallway toward the front room. She listened at the closed sliding doors. The table lamp was still on, and the sighing could clearly be heard. And the sound of a glass being set down on the bedside table.

Then Ika remembered the beakers of milk still sitting on the tray. She'd completely forgotten. Would Mother be thirsty? Should she make her a cup of tea?

But it didn't happen. The sliding doors were either locked or jammed, for Ika couldn't get them open. She returned to her room upstairs, surprised that in such a short time she had become very cold.

She lay there waiting, longing for the first bird to be heard outside her window on the roof's gutter. Just as she always used to wait.

## CHAPTER TWELVE

THE DEW LAY IN round droplets on the leaves of the lady's mantle. The light was a golden autumn light. Ika took deep breaths of the morning air. The early morning sun felt warm on her face. She looked up into the blue sky.

Mother would talk today. Things would go better than yesterday. Something new must turn up. She must not be so timid about asking questions. And she must persist, not thinking about herself, but putting Mother first. She had not come here for nothing. Maybe there wasn't much time left. Dealing with Mother was similar to dealing with the winter garden. Something had to open up. Something had to be born.

So Ika concluded that the day, their conversation, their relationship must start with her. What sense was there in waiting and expecting something from Mother? Ika decided she should just go into the front room and give Mother a kiss. This was her first job. But it was so difficult.

She made tea and then buttered some *beschuit*, or zwieback toast, placing thin slices of cheese on them—an old favorite of Mother's.

She'd been at the farm all day. The cowshed had to be scrubbed out. The day before, the cows had gone out to pasture in a state of mad excitement. Aaltje had invited her.

"I don't know what you see in it," Mother had said. "Such a stinking mess."

But Ika had danced with the cows. It was fun scrubbing down the cowshed. She used the big hose and sprayed the floor and walls, then scrubbed it with a broom, over and over till all the filth was gone. And at the end of the afternoon when the cowshed was dripping and shining clean, everyone would be dead tired but pleased for having accomplished something.

Ika was working alongside adults and she wanted to show them she could work. The others might complain about their backs, but she wouldn't, even though she sometimes felt like it.

Aaltje had tied a knot in Ika's wide skirt so it wouldn't get wet. Ika ran around in Aaltje's black Wellington boots with her skinny knees just showing over the tops of the boots. Ika tried to be careful, but soon she was sopping wet. Even her hair hung in wet streamers around her face. It wasn't meant to happen, but the hard stream of water had rebounded in a fountain against the corners of the drain.

It was already five o'clock when Aaltje shouted that the coffee was ready. Ika got some, too, though hers was nearly white with milk. Her teeth chattered against the rim of the cup, as her ice-cold hands came back to life again.

Ika was hoping for a thick slice of gingerbread slab cake. It seemed Aaltje was a mind reader because she stood up saying she was going to see about finding some slab cake to have with the coffee. Halfway into her search, Aaltje turned and shouted, "Or would you rather have some zwieback toast and cheese?"

*Mother loves zwieback and cheese*, Ika thought in a flash. Ika didn't like it much herself, but she could keep hers for Mother. "Yes, I'd rather have the zwieback toast!"

When Aaltje set them in front of her, Ika had to work hard to keep from eating. She was very hungry after all the scrubbing, yet she stuck to her decision. It was nice to have a surprise for Mother. What would Mother say when she suddenly presented it from behind her back?

On the way home Ika noticed that the zwieback had gotten a little soggy. She was so wet herself. She tried to blow the bread dry, but it didn't work.

Mother was standing peeling beets, her hands all red. She repeatedly blew a piece of straggly hair away from in front of her eyes.

Ika walked over and stood quietly behind her and, with excitement in her voice, said, "Mum, just guess what I've brought you!"

Mother's shoulders moved. "I wouldn't know."

From behind her back, Ika produced a folded napkin that held the zwieback and cheese. It looked wet. While looking up at

Mother, she set the napkin on the kitchen counter beside the saucepan of beets.

"What's that?" Mother asked.

"Zwieback toast with a bit of cheese, that's all. One of your favorite snacks, right?"

"Where did you get it?"

Ika studied her face. Mother didn't seem to like what she'd done. Disappointment welled up inside her. Deflated, Ika said quietly, "I got it from Aaltje. I could choose slab cake or the zwieback toast. I thought I'd take the zwieback . . . for you."

Mother dropped a beet into the pan. A red splash hit her just under the eye. She rubbed the place with her hand, but this made it even worse so she went to wash her face under the tap. Afterward she said, "It was very sweet of you to think of me."

It looked as if she'd been crying. This probably wasn't the case, however, because Mother didn't cry so easily. Nonetheless, it had given Ika an odd, restless feeling, like she had somehow hurt her mother.

Mother was sleeping when Ika came into the front room. She set the tea on the bedside table and then quietly pulled aside the curtains. The room came alive when Ika opened the window. Sitting down quietly on the edge of the bed, she watched her mother's mouth. Mother was making tiny sounds as she breathed in and out. Relaxed, it was a beautiful mouth, still young looking.

Mother was now fifty-three, a young age to die.

Had Ika inherited her mother's mouth? She didn't know. Nelly's mouth was different. She suppressed the urge to go and look in the mirror. What did it matter if she had Mother's mouth or not?

She moistened her lips with her tongue and kissed her own hand. That was how she had to do the kiss. It was nothing. She sighed deeply and bent over toward Mother's cheek. The smell of the sickroom filled her senses. It included the smell of the ointment for the bedsores. Mother's skin felt warm and dry to her lips. Her heart raced in a funny way when she sat up straight again. Mother's eyes were now open.

"I've made some tea," said Ika.

Mother averted her eyes and tried to straighten herself. Without thinking, Ika followed the ritual with Mother's pillows, fluffing them up behind her back. The silence from outside seemed to filter into the room—a healthy silence, without any words. Ika handed the plate with the zwieback to her, and Mother took tiny bites. Her munching made the silence even more intense. Was Mother now thinking about the other slice of zwieback toast? Ika smiled over the teapot, as Mother paused in her movement and nodded.

A car drove by and then everything became quiet again. Ika glanced over at the alarm clock. It was still only half past seven. "Does the nurse come every day?"

Mother shook her head and, when she had swallowed the little bit of food she'd been chewing, said, "Only on Tuesdays and Fridays." Then she paused and looked confused. "It *is* Wednesday today, isn't it?"

Ika nodded and smiled. In the early stillness, being there didn't seem so difficult anymore. But one never knew with Mother how long this would last. "Would you like me to wash you now?" Mother looked at her blankly. There was so little to see in her eyes, only pain really, which had pushed away all other emotion. "Or would you rather wait for Nelly?" Ika nervously clasped her hands together. "I promise to be careful. Just tell me how I should do it." She then stood in front of the closet and took out Mother's underclothes. "Do you want the blue nightie here or the flannel one?"

But Mother made no reply. She pushed the plate away and folded her hands. She lay for a long time with her eyes closed. Ika saw her from the mirror hanging on the inside of the closet door. She remained still, watching until Mother opened her eyes again. Their eyes met in the mirror. "Just give me the blue one."

Suddenly Mother's eyes looked different, as if the mirror allowed Ika to look through the pain. Ika was flustered by what she saw. For her mother's eyes were filled with such loneliness, as though she'd been lying in that bed all her life and hadn't met another human being. They spoke of a woman devoid of real conversation and companionship, as if there was no chance now for her to connect with another person.

Ika turned around, laid the nightie on the bed, and sat down close beside her. Now the eyes were as they had been—pained eyes.

An icy fear shot through Ika as she allowed herself to think about the fact that Mother would die. Nobody knew how soon. "Should I get water? And then after you're washed I'll make some coffee, like yesterday."

Smoothing down the sheet with her hand, Mother looked away from her. "Why should you stay?"

"Because I want to look after you," said Ika, despite the increasing pain in her chest. "Because you are ill, and somebody has to look after you."

"There's Nelly."

"But Nelly has her own family. She can't always be here." Ika stood up. The pain was unbearable, but when she leaned down to pick up the washbowl, she said it. "You're *my* mother too!" And a little later in the kitchen, while the noise of the stream of water drowned out the sound of her heavy sobbing, what she really wanted to say finally came out: "*I'm* your daughter too!"

How could this hurt so much? In spite of the tears she couldn't control, Ika walked back to the sickroom. She pulled back the sheet, undressed Mother, and washed her with a tenderness that had begun to grow after the pain of sobbing. She patted the bedsores dry while using the hair-dryer and then applied the ointment. She combed Mother's hair and clipped a nail that was beginning to snag. The tenderness endured as if Mother were a child, only in a position to receive, too helpless even to return a smile.

As Ika was dumping out the wash water, she suddenly cried, "O Lord!" For the tenderness that had sprung up after her crying had made her feel warm and soft inside. Such tenderness was something new to her. She sang with the water that was singing in the kettle. There was the smell of coffee. And outside she could hear the song of the titmouse again—tee-cha, tee-cha, tee-cha. Ika pulled open the kitchen door to hear it better.

When Nelly was born, Ika had stood amazed at the cradle for days. It remained her earliest memory—the little doll that was breathing so quietly with those dainty hands sticking out of the tiny cotton sweater. The little red legs emerging from a soft diaper with its pink edging. Experiencing such a wonder, one of God's wonders, had captivated her young heart.

But Mother was lying in bed with blood red eyes. Dr. Spaan had said that this was what the stork had done.

"Was she pecked at?" Ika had asked with an anxious, trembling voice.

"Maybe she was," he'd said. "But she'll get better soon."

Grandmother came and, in her slow quiet way, she looked after the household. When Ika voiced her concern about Mother's eyes Grandmother calmed her down, telling Ika not to worry. She said that it wasn't because of the stork, but because of the baby. And it wasn't important. Sometimes this happened when a baby was born.

Ika accepted her grandmother's explanation without question. Anyway, she had never seen a stork.

"Is she staying?" Ika had asked Mother one day as Mother was feeding Nelly.

Mother nodded, then looked up from the baby toward Ika.

"Always?"

"Always. Are you pleased?"

Ika laid her hand on Nelly's little tummy, close to Mother's breast. With a gentle finger, she felt the sucking and the swallowing.

"Yes, because now I've got a little sister. Are you pleased too?"

Mother was so beautiful when she smiled like that.

The telephone made a sound from another world. Surprised, Ika went to answer it and found it in the hall. It was Simone, abrupt as she always was when she was scared to let her emotions show.

Was her mother still alive? And had Ika begun designing the winter garden yet?

Ika leaned against the wall with her eyes closed, so as not to be obliged to look down the hallway. She said that she was fine and that she'd slept in her old bed. As for the winter garden, she asked if Simone had thought about a supplier for the tiles.

"No," said Simone. "That's your job. I suppose you've already thought of somebody?"

"Not really," Ika replied. "I've hardly gotten started."

"Can you work there?" Simone sounded skeptical.

"I'm so glad you called. You don't need to worry. Everything's going okay, really."

"I'm not worried, but I did have a rotten night. You were haunting me."

Ika could almost see Simone's face in front of her. She knew what she looked like when she said such things. Ika smiled and started talking again, about the tiles for paving the winter garden. "I was thinking we should get the tiles from Van Leeuwen's. They've got a wide assortment to choose from."

"Are you crazy!" Simone said sharply. "That man nearly ruined us with the playground. He took us for a ride with his delivery times and then swindled us afterward. Whatever gave you that idea, anyway?"

"Even so, I could at least ask him for an estimate."

"But why go back to him? Aren't there any others? Have they brainwashed you or something?"

"Maybe Van Leeuwen's would make it up to you. You should give him another chance to do it. Some people can't do that of their own accord."

It was quiet for a while, then finally Simone sighed. "Just remember to keep it businesslike. We've not all been struck by your 'here's a chance to make good' virus."

"Great," said Ika. "I still have his number, so I'll go ahead and contact him. Thanks for calling, Simone, and don't go and kick the filing cabinet. You might break your toes!"

The sun was shining through the little hall window, and it conjured up a green-and-blue mosaic on the floor.

## CHAPTER THIRTEEN

THE DOVE CALLED AS Ika was opening his little door. With the bird on her shoulder, she prepared her drawing board.

The day enticed her to work, but first she'd have to put down on paper her ideas from yesterday evening. She drew in the lines for the garden and indicated the entrance. The dove cooed as he watched her movements.

The wind picked up and began tugging at the window, so Ika went over and closed it. The weather was changing. Great billowing clouds had spread across the blue sky. On and off, the sun shone brightly through the window in a crooked stripe over her drawing board. Just as she thought to move her work to a more favorable position in the light, another cloud would appear to dull the lighting on the paper.

As regards shade, Ika had to take into account the low winter sun, which would cast long shadows. Such a detail determined how she'd lay out the garden. For how something looked depended on how the light fell on it and also on the position from which one looked. It seemed to Ika to be a rule that applied to everything in life.

She must remember to put the coffee on.

Soon Nelly's quick steps could be heard coming around the back. When she came in, with her came a blast of cold air and the smell of outside, of manure.

"They're at it again," Nelly commented, hanging up her coat. "I don't mind this village, but that everlasting stink!"

"Really? Well, as far as I'm concerned you can leave the door open."

"What's that dove doing loose? If you keep carrying on like that, you'll get it looking in here like the muckheap it is outside."

"And what's with you this morning? Get out of the wrong side of bed?" Ika inquired dryly.

"Sorry, just having my period. Nothing else." Nelly's half smile grew broader as she looked at Ika. She made a movement as if to shake something off. "I know all about it. I'm just like Mother in that respect—crabby. Are you too?"

Ika laughed, for she was taken a little aback that Nelly could speak so casually of things that used to be unmentionable. "No, I just get a headache," she said curtly.

"So how did it go? Did Mother sleep for a bit? How about you?"

Ika told her there was nothing to report. Then she put the coffee on while Nelly went to see Mother.

The faint sound of Mother's and Nelly's voices drifted as far as the kitchen. Ika couldn't understand the words, but the conversation sounded reproachful on both sides.

When Ika walked in with the coffee, Nelly was treating the bed-sores on Mother's back. Ika wanted to tell her that she'd just seen to them. However, the look in Nelly's eyes and the subtle gesture with her head made her hold back. Ika understood that Mother had made it clear to Nelly that she was indispensable, and also that Nelly had no wish to quarrel about it.

"Does Ika know that Aunt Klaar is coming this afternoon?" asked Nelly, while carefully dabbing a bedsore.

Mother's face grew somber. "I don't want to see Klaar. She can stay away, along with all her endless stories about the past."

Nelly told Mother firmly that she wasn't being fair. Aunt Klaar came faithfully every Wednesday afternoon and she should appreciate this.

Shrugging her shoulders, Mother said, "Since I've become ill, I have to appreciate everything, but nobody listens to what I want."

"Would you like some coffee?" Ika cut in. She got a hard impatient nod.

Nelly just shook her head.

Aunt Klaar was Father's only sister. She was ten years younger and had remained unmarried. She knew everyone because she'd been a seamstress for what seemed like the whole world. She would go to their houses, and because of her bold curiosity, she learned almost everything about people.

During the times when Aunt Klaar came to sew—one day in the spring for new summer dresses, and one day in the autumn for winter skirts—Mother would make something extra special to eat. Aunt Klaar loved Mother's tasty cooking, and she ate a lot of it. In exchange for the meals, after a day of talking with Aunt Klaar, Mother was completely in the know about all the bits of gossip in the village and surrounding neighborhood.

Ika and Nelly were always excited to hear Aunt Klaar was coming over, even though they had little to say in the choice of style or fabric. Mother left this all up to their aunt. With a deft hand she would cut fronts and backs from large rolls of cloth that often looked like each other, and always counterclockwise. Aunt Klaar had it in her mind that, because she was left-handed, this was the better way.

On one such occasion, when a winter coat had to be made for Ika, Aunt Klaar came to fetch her to go into town and look for some cloth. But Ika was embarrassed when with Aunt Klaar in public. Often while riding in the bus, her aunt would speak to anyone and everyone. Ika should have enjoyed the trip to town, yet she mostly longed to get back home, and quickly. Aunt Klaar's boisterous voice, and the way she kept going on about things that didn't concern her, made Ika feel sick.

Everyone in the fabric shop knew her aunt Klaar. Those that worked there would sit her down in a chair and give her a cup of coffee, something they didn't typically do for their customers.

On that day, Aunt Klaar asked about a checked material, and while the shop assistant was busy gathering a pile of colored samples in the most horrible combinations, Ika had found for herself the cloth she wanted for her coat. The cloth was green and would do perhaps for a duffle coat. It had to have big pockets.

In between sips of her coffee, Aunt Klaar brought the shop assistant up-to-date with her stories, and Ika stood there the whole time, wondering how she could possibly persuade her auntie that her coat had to be made of the green cloth she held in her hand.

"Who's she?" asked the woman from the shop, nodding in Ika's direction.

"Surely I told you about her." Then Klaar's voice dropped to a whisper. "It's the girl from my sister-in-law. You know, the minister's daughter. The storm has died down a bit now, but goodness knows there was an awful fuss about it."

The woman glanced again at Ika and then raised her eyebrows at Aunt Klaar.

"I'd like this material, Aunt Klaar," Ika said as she pushed the mound of checked samples aside.

Klaar laid a hand on Ika's shoulder, yet kept looking at the shop assistant. "The chance-child the minister called Ikabod. My brother was keen on the girl for years, but she never told anyone whose it was. Didn't you know?"

The shop bell rang, and Ika breathed again with a sigh of relief. The woman had to serve another customer.

"Aunt Klaar, I don't want a checked coat. I want this green material. Can you make me a duffle coat with this?"

Klaar, easily moved as she was, had found it all quite pathetic. "Poor lamb. Of course I'll make you a duffle coat with that, and with real wooden toggles."

But it was a coat with a secret, for Ika knew that "chance-child" meant something bad, as Aunt Klaar didn't whisper very often. She usually said things loudly.

Things hadn't been very good between Mother and Aunt Klaar, though there was never an improper word that passed between them. It was like it always was with Mother. The fighting was carried out with looks and gestures, or worse, by being silent and ignoring the other person.

So Klaar was coming that afternoon. Ika admitted to Nelly that she was curious about her aunt. Nelly expected that they'd soon be fed up with her rattling on. The gossiping hadn't gotten any better—actually quite the opposite.

Back in the dining room, Ika whispered tentatively to Nelly, "Do you know it was from Aunt Klaar that I learned Mother wasn't married when I was born?"

"How old were you then?"

"Twelve. It was in the fabric shop on Bree Street."

"Honestly? In public?" Nelly sympathized.

"Klaar whispered it to the shop assistant, while I was standing there looking on."

"That's terrible! Though that's what she's always been like."

Nelly took out the vacuum cleaner and began to vacuum the room, but her thoughts were obviously still on their conversation. Before long she switched off the machine and asked, "Had you not realized it before then?"

"No, I did think it was strange that I was older than the number of years Mother and Father had been married. Even so, I never thought anymore about it at the time. I had no idea what was involved in having a baby."

"If I recall, you weren't at all curious about those things," said Nelly with a laugh. "I believe even I knew all about having babies then. You were more interested in fairy stories than I was. Besides, I was a friend of Carien's, remember? She told me lots of things I'd never heard before."

They both burst out laughing. Yes, Carien always did everything before anyone else had done it.

"Do you ever see her?"

"Seldom. And then only in the supermarket. She's divorced now, has a son of seventeen. She still looks like a little doll with those dark curls. Oh, and it was her mother's fault that Carien was more *forward* than we were."

"Mean people called Mother that, do you remember? Where did she get the nerve for it, unless she herself after all—"

"Quiet, Ika," Nelly said with a rebuking tone.

They stared at each other with the same question in their eyes.

"Do you know who it was?" asked Ika.

"No. Nobody ever talked about it."

Then Mother's voice interrupted them. Ika stepped through the sliding doors to see what she wanted.

"Are you two going to stay talking to each other all day and leave me lying here on my own?"

"We're cleaning the place up. Then it will be all nice for when Aunt Klaar comes later on," Ika said while maintaining a straight face.

When she came back into the kitchen, Nelly's eyes twinkled. All at once they were conspirators together.

"Perhaps it was a rape after all," said Nelly.

"I don't think so," Ika said. "If it was rape, then it wouldn't have had to be such a secret the whole time. Mother would've been able to talk about it by now."

"Do you really want to know?"

"That's why I came. When Mother's no longer with us, there'll be nobody else to tell me. This is my last chance."

A look of disappointment entered Nelly's eyes. After a pause, she asked, "What do you think of Abe?"

Ika turned around. "Abe? He's . . . I can't find the words to describe him. He's . . . wonderful. Is the other one like that too?"

While Ika spoke enthusiastically, Nelly couldn't help but chuckle. "The other one's quite a different story. You'll find all that out later. He's coming here at twelve o'clock, as it's Wednesday."

"And Abe too?"

Nelly shook her head and said, "Wednesday afternoons he usually goes to see Willem's father. He enjoys all that farming business. That's just how he is."

"Then he's got more of me in him than just the gardening."

Ika turned to the drawing board. The outline of the garden was sketched in, but her idea with the embrace still had to be worked out. Paths of flagstones or fluorspar pebbles, which should it be? Ika envisioned yellow fluorspar pebbles with moss growing between them, flanked by skimmias and standard viburnum, with winter-flowering jasmine in the background along the inside wall.

Nelly walked over and stood behind her. "Ika, what are you working on? Is this for your work?"

"Yes. I'm planning a winter garden for a hotel. It's a big commission for us."

"A winter garden? I can't imagine what that would look like, but it sounds beautiful. A winter garden sounds like something out of a fairy tale."

"It will be a fairy tale," Ika promised.

"How do you get the ideas? Does it always turn out as you thought when you drew up the plans?"

"That depends. Some projects are easier than others. But the more intricate the design and the more you get absorbed into it, the more insight seems to come. I find that I have to walk through the garden in my imagination, to find beautiful things there or discover the flaws that need to be corrected."

"Abe would like your job."

"One day, when the garden's ready," said Ika, measuring out a line exactly to the millimeter, "if it turns out as I want it to, perhaps he'll be able to come along and have a look. I could even pick him up or something . . . if you'd allow that."

"So you haven't come back just for the past," Nelly said quietly.

"I think Abe's really great, and Willem's a hundred percent okay too. And . . . it's been good to see you again." Finally Ika looked up at Nelly as if Nelly owed her a reply. But Nelly said nothing. Ika only noticed the little wrinkles around her eyes, as if she was on the verge of laughing. "Sometimes you ask for one thing and get another," Ika said, giving a quick shrug.

Nelly stifled a laugh and said, "But you don't know what I was asking."

Aunt Klaar gave lessons in knitting and embroidery, otherwise known as *Useful Needlecraft*, at Ika's school. From the third grade and up, students were allowed to spend one hour per week in

Klaar's classroom, located at the very end of the corridor. Walking this corridor gave Ika a special feeling of freedom as she passed class after class of children who were bent over their exercise books, working hard.

Ika noticed that her aunt was much stricter at school than at home, and that Aunt Klaar had the habit of looking somewhat grim-faced when in the classroom, as though bracing herself in case something dreadful occurred.

Ika disliked the knitting. Her hands always got clammy, and the cotton washcloth she had to knit became a stiff, shapeless thing that couldn't be pushed backward or forward on the rusty needles. Most of the time she couldn't get the grubby white thread to go around the needle correctly. So she went and stood in line with the others, waiting her turn to get help.

Aunt Klaar, who was called *Miss* at school, would often complain about her students' lack of skill before demonstrating the correct method in her odd left-handed way. Somehow she always got the obstinate knitting loose again. *Why is it that I can't knit any better?* Ika would lament. *Mother could knit just as well without even trying.*

One day, just as it was Ika's turn to get help, the principal entered the classroom. His appearing like this didn't happen very much. Aunt Klaar sat up straight, while Ika held her knitting behind her back.

The principal's stern eyes surveyed the class. Then he smiled, and the children breathed again, showing their relief.

"Miss de Haan," the principal said as he stuck out his huge hand, "what do you think I have here in my hand?"

"I don't know," said Klaar nervously.

He opened his hand to reveal a button. It was a button belonging apparently to his jacket. "I got it caught in the closet. Might one of these hardworking needlewomen be able to repair my jacket?"

Immediately a few hands shot up. "Miss, me! I can do it, please!"

Aunt Klaar lifted the needle case and removed a needle. She then cut a long thread from a spool and poked the thread through the needle's eye. In the meantime she glanced across the rows of students.

*Who would it be? Would she sew it herself?*

The principal took off his jacket, and the children all giggled at the sight of his bulging suspenders.

Then Aunt Klaar fixed her gaze on Ika. Almost imperceptibly, Ika shook her head as if to say, "Not me, not me!"

But Aunt Klaar kept looking at her and asked, "Ika, would you be able to do it?"

Ika held out her bungled knitting and shrugged. Aunt Klaar smiled, then took the knitting away. So with her face glowing red, Ika picked up the principal's jacket. It felt warm and smelled like a cigar.

She was told to sit in the big chair. The principal stood waiting beside her, while the entire class watched Ika closely as she attempted to sew the button back on.

Ika returned to her seat when she'd finished, still showing a flush in her cheeks and neck. The principal thanked her twice. For, although Ika couldn't knit too well yet, she could sew a button with great skill. And Aunt Klaar seemed to know this.

Nelly had opened the door, and as Aunt Klaar was removing her coat in the hall, she announced before hardly saying hello that the village baker was getting divorced. When she recognized Ika, her eyeglasses misted up.

Ika had been waiting where she could see herself reflected in the glass of the china cabinet.

"Child!" said Aunt Klaar, pressing Ika to her ample bosom. But Ika didn't respond very cooperatively. "Ika, my child, fancy me meeting you here at home now! I often think about you. How are you keeping?"

Ika gave her aunt a kiss back, feeling pleased she'd followed Nelly's advice and baked a cake.

Aunt Klaar walked through to the front room, still acting surprised by Ika's being there. Greeting Mother, she said, "Well then, you must be very happy that Ika's here."

"Hello, Klaar," Mother replied. "Imagine you coming out in this strong wind."

"It was better than I'd expected. With a bit of sunshine it was easy enough. And I walked here. I get so breathless on the bike. When did Ika come?"

"Yesterday," said Mother reluctantly.

But Aunt Klaar didn't notice the reluctance. She seized Mother's arm and demanded, "So how did Ika hear you were sick? How long is she staying?"

"That I don't know, Klaar, and you mustn't make such a fuss. Remember, you're visiting the sick."

Ika went ahead and cut slices of the still-warm cake, measuring out a thick one for her aunt Klaar.

"Should I?" Klaar hesitated, her eyes fastened on the large piece.

"Go on," said Ika. "Enjoy."

"All right then!"

It was a pleasure to see her auntie eating. Nelly gave Ika a wink.

As soon as Klaar could think of new questions, the cross-examination began. "Now, just tell me, child . . ."

Ika answered with few words, yet Aunt Klaar persisted with more and more questions. About her work. About whether perhaps she had a boyfriend, saying, "You could still get one." Or about her house, and whether she still attended church.

Now and then Mother would intervene, looking for some attention. Once she asked straight out which of them Klaar had come to see.

Nelly was right. The entertainment was soon over. Ika was glad when Aunt Klaar stood up, because for the second time Mother had warned Klaar that she'd better get home before the roads got too busy.

When they were washing the cups afterward, Nelly commented, "She asked everything Mother wanted to know."

"Yes, I suppose so," Ika said.

## CHAPTER FOURTEEN

MOTHER HAD A FEVER. She lay there burning hot with strange glazed eyes. It gave Ika and Nelly a feeling of guilt. Had they not given Mother enough attention?

Nelly phoned home, as it seemed better if Dirk-Willem didn't come. Too many people in the house might be overwhelming for Mother.

Ika could hear his small rattling voice on the other end of the telephone. Nelly acting as mother, soothing and organizing things, was a lovely sight to behold. After she hung up, a blanket of silence fell over the household.

Nelly wondered whether or not she should call Dr. Spaan. "I'll stay here tonight," she said.

Ika nodded. Their dinner had remained untouched in the saucepans. Nobody was hungry.

Then Willem came to the back door, and Nelly went to meet him there. Ika could hear their muffled voices while she stayed with Mother, bathing her forehead with a wet washcloth. Even Willem was speaking softly now.

She studied her mother's languid face. Her breathing was quick and shallow. Her chest hardly moved. But on her temple there was a vein visible, beating fast and angrily. Ika stroked the sheet smooth again and picked up Mother's hand to feel her pulse. The hand felt dry and wrinkled as it lay quietly in hers. "Mother, would you like something more to drink?"

A feeble movement showed that indeed Mother had heard the question, but that she didn't want anything.

Much like a sigh, the word *pain* slipped from her thin lips.

"Your back," Ika said, bending over her.

"Pain . . . everywhere," she whispered.

Mother's eyes appeared to sink away into their sockets. Suddenly she appeared very old and nearing her end.

"You've got to call the doctor," Ika said when Nelly stepped noiselessly into the room.

Nelly just nodded.

"She's in a lot of pain. Can she have a pain-killer now?"

"Those hardly help her anymore. She's been taking them for weeks. Maybe Dr. Spaan has something stronger."

Ika looked down at Mother. "I hope so."

Under her closed eyelids Mother's eyes moved quickly, and a nervous twitch shot along her mouth.

"Let's take her temperature again," said Nelly.

In her eyes was the same anxiety, the same knowledge.

Dr. Spaan arrived a little before nine that night. Nelly waited at the front door as he was getting out of his car.

"Well . . ." he said to the thermometer before he shook it. Mother didn't seem to realize he was there. Her eyes were barely open.

Dr. Spaan sank down onto the bed, causing it to creak noisily. He looked at her and skimmed his hand over her face, as if he meant that Mother should close her eyes again. The gesture brought a lump to Ika's throat. It was the gesture of a father. It was then that Ika saw how very highly Dr. Spaan thought of her mother.

He straightened himself up and then bent over and stroked her hair a couple of times. Around his mouth was a look of apology. Beckoning Ika and Nelly to follow him to the back room, Dr. Spaan later said, "This isn't good. If the fever persists, then I'm afraid she won't last much longer. Her body can't cope. And what about you two? Can you deal with these final days?"

Nelly gripped Ika's arm. "What should we expect, Doctor?"

The way he shrugged his shoulders said it all. Again he asked, "Can you deal with this?"

"We'll sit up tonight together," Ika said with a glance toward Nelly.

"And tomorrow?" His countenance seemed sterner now.

"Tomorrow too," said Ika.

"It'll be very difficult. She could become confused. May want to get out of bed. And she'll probably get angry with you."

"Mother has expressed she wants to stay at home till the end," Nelly pleaded. "I think we've got to honor her wish. It's the last thing we can do for her."

The flicker of a smile crossed his features. "Of course. I won't stand in your way. I'm only explaining what the situation entails. I'll come back tomorrow morning before going into a surgery I have scheduled. See you then."

Nelly went to follow him into the hall, but before she got there the doctor had already shut the door behind him and was walking out to his car.

Ika leaned against the sliding door. As she looked at Mother from a distance, she looked dead already. The gray of her face stood out above the white of the sheets.

The little bottle filled with Mother's pain tablets rattled in Ika's hand. She looked at it, then at Nelly who was crying.

"It's going to happen, Ika. I'm so glad you're here."

"You've got Willem and the boys as well." Ika wasn't sure what had made her say this. Did she want to keep some distance between them, to keep out of harm's way?

Nelly walked into the kitchen to bathe her eyes. Ika could hardly hear what she was saying over the sound of the running water. "I'm talking about you now. You must understand that."

Ika went to check on Mother. She gently moved the hair from her face and adjusted the sheets. Returning from the kitchen, Nelly came and stood beside the bed.

"We're both here, Mother. *We* are with you."

"Do you remember the time you had diphtheria?" Ika turned to Nelly and held out her hand. "Then it was Mother and I sitting here with you."

Nelly bent over and felt Mother's throat. "I can only remember it after I'd gotten better, when all my clothes were too big. I had lost so much weight with the fever. Do you remember how high my temperature was?"

Ika handed the tablets to Nelly who opened the bottle at once.

It was winter and no matter how warm Mother tried to make the back room, the windowpanes in the front room were resplendent with patterns of frost. The stove in the front room couldn't be used, for too much heat wasn't good for Nelly.

Nelly had diphtheria, which turned out to be as bad as it sounded. Ika had repeated the word ten times quietly. *Diphtheria.* The word sounded like some sort of poison to Ika. Dr. Spaan had told her that Nelly's sickness was like a poison—one that had infected her throat. This was why it was so hard for Nelly to swallow. The poison was also behind her eyes, so Nelly couldn't see so well either.

All day long Mother sat by Nelly's bed, tightly holding her hand. She kept calling Nelly's name as if she was afraid Nelly might go away.

"Mother, she hasn't got any shoes on," Ika had said. "She can't go away. And she's only wearing her nightie." But Mother didn't hear Ika.

Father had begun coming home early from work to see Nelly. "How is she?" he'd ask while pulling off his boots at the back door.

"Still sick, and she still can't drink," Ika would say.

No meals were cooked, as Mother had no time for this. The baker brought loaves of bread, and Father made sandwiches on the kitchen counter. Always with cheese.

And after they had eaten, Ika had to go straight to bed so that she wouldn't get sick too. She wasn't allowed to kiss Nelly, nor did Mother or Father give her any kisses.

Going to bed by herself had felt strange to Ika. She would walk alone down the hall and then up the stairs. With the darkness behind her back, the trip to her room was scary. And nobody came to look in on her later. It seemed there was only Nelly in the family, and that she was invisible.

One morning Ika had gone downstairs very early. It was still dark outside. Mother lay sleeping on the chair with her mouth open. She was nearly falling out of the chair. The table lamp was still on.

Ika tiptoed into the front room, sat down on Nelly's bed, and, just like Mother, stroked her face. Nelly opened her eyes yet didn't seem to be looking at anything. "*I'm* here Nelly," said Ika, like her mother. "I'm still here."

Nelly moved her mouth as if she didn't know whether to laugh or cry. Ika caressed her head and hair. She felt so warm. It was awful for Nelly, this pain, and that she couldn't swallow without hurting.

Ika wove her fingers through Nelly's.

They should pray. People have to pray when they're in need. Grandfather had said so in church. " 'Pray without ceasing. Ask and it will be given unto you. Seek and ye shall find,' " he'd shouted from the pulpit, his hands held high above his head. There was also something about knocking on a door, but Ika wasn't exactly sure about this part.

*Maybe praying is like knocking on God's door*, she mused, *which was another good reason to pray.*

"Lord, bless this food." *This sounded very poor*, Ika thought. "Lord, bless this food. Lord, bless this food. Lord, bless this food. Lord, thanks for this food. Lord, thanks for this food."

Food was pain. A sort of pain like Nelly's. God would know this. She must knock on His door. Ika began to pray more and more loudly. She pressed her eyes tightly shut, remembering she must always be reverent before the Lord. Yet all the while she kept her face pointing in Nelly's direction.

Suddenly the chair creaked, and a hand grasped her shoulder before she had a chance to look up.

"Child, how could you? Mocking the Lord like that and with your little sick sister."

Ika let go of Nelly and shrank backward until she felt the frost patterns pressing against her back, seeping through her nightie.

Then for the first time in days, Nelly spoke an intelligible word. She whispered, "Thirsty . . ."

Mother quickly fetched a cup of water. Her hand shook as she brought it close to Nelly's lips, so that she spilled some of it onto the bed sheet. "Nelly, drink up. Drink up. Drink up!" Mother urged.

Her telling Nelly to drink up sounded to Ika like when she prayed "Lord, bless this food."

The coldness Ika felt on her back helped against the warm feeling behind her eyes. Her throat also felt strange. Would she become like Nelly and not be able to swallow anymore?

She kept trying to swallow till finally her mouth went dry and her neck muscles hurt. Later, when she had forgotten about it for a while, her throat felt normal again. Perhaps she hadn't mocked the Lord as badly as Mother had thought.

The curtains were closed in the front room, where they sat watching Mother sleep. So the lamp glowing from the back room through the stained glass doors was the only light in the room. It was dark enough for Nelly and Ika to talk about things they couldn't readily say aloud in the daylight.

Nelly began. "Why did you not come to Father's funeral?"

Ika remained silent.

"Mother was very disappointed that you didn't come."

"Did she say that then?" Ika asked in a half whisper.

"No, of course not. She would've bitten her tongue off to avoid bringing up your name."

"Exactly."

Nelly turned to face Ika. "Did you hate Father so much that you didn't even want to say a final good-bye to him?"

"I haven't thought much about my feelings concerning him. I always focused more on what he thought of me. And that wasn't very good, Nelly. I can't remember getting a kind word or approving look from him . . . ever. With him, I felt like I didn't exist. I believe the neighbor's dog meant more to him than me. He barely tolerated me in this house."

Nelly sighed and pushed her chair back so she could see Ika better. "If he couldn't stand you, then why did he marry Mother?"

"That's what I'd like to know. I was eighteen months old when they married. I have no idea what was happening at that time."

Mother moved her head restlessly against the pillow. Ika stood and walked over to the bed. "What is it, Mother? Would you like a drink of something?"

She looked up at Ika with an anguished expression on her face, not really seeing Ika, then pushed the straw impatiently away.

Ika took a fresh wet washcloth and placed it gently against Mother's mouth. Mother's eyes closed slowly as she sucked the water from the washcloth with minute jerks. Ika dribbled more water onto it, as a feeling of tenderness welled up inside her. "Go on, Mother, draw out the water. Good. A little bit more."

Nelly was moved by Ika's sensitivity toward Mother. What did she and Ika even know of each other? Nothing really. Where had she gotten the courage to write to Ika that she should come? And why had Ika come? Nelly got up and stepped into the hallway to escape the soft voice and the sucking noise that seemed to make Mother even weaker. She pressed her face into the folds of Mother's coat that was hanging pointlessly on the hallstand. The coat still smelled of Mother.

"What are you doing, Nelly?" Ika flipped the light on, and the hall was instantly filled with a harsh brightness. They both blinked. "What is it? Are you crying?"

Nelly shook her head, but then began to weep. She spoke incomprehensibly between the sobs, words about Willem and her boys and that she thought it was so sad that she, Ika, lived all alone.

"Sister, dear . . . come on now," said Ika, astonished. Then grabbing Nelly's hand, she said, "You must be crazy. Why should you go worrying yourself over me? Especially at a time like this." They both had to laugh.

The embrace that followed had all the time been waiting to come. They were the same height, though Nelly was rounder and softer. Ika didn't know whose tears she'd tasted when they started to laugh again.

The moment felt surreal, as surreal as Mother lying on her deathbed in the front room.

## CHAPTER FIFTEEN

IT HAD BEEN A LONG NIGHT. They had lost all track of time.

When morning finally came, Ika and Nelly felt as though they had been sitting beside Mother's bed for a week, listening anxiously to her unsteady breathing. On a couple of occasions all was quiet for a bit, during which times they would hold their breath until Mother resumed her faltering pattern of breathing. She hardly had the strength to clear her throat, and coughing was all but impossible.

Mother would open her eyes periodically, and then Nelly would try to get through to her by taking her hand and calling her name. Yet, the few times Mother said something back, her words were mostly an incomprehensible mumbling. Still, Mother stayed quite calm, her uneasiness kept internal for the most part. They could see this from the way her eyes went back and forth under their lids, from the way she gripped the sheet, the expressions on her mouth.

She refused to get out of bed, no longer desiring things she felt were impossible. Instead she appeared to be sinking deeper and deeper into another place. Sometimes it seemed Mother was suddenly realizing this fact and she would take hold of the sheet or Nelly's hand as if grasping for something to buoy her. If Ika relieved Nelly at the bedside, still within hand's reach, Mother seemed to notice, for then the sheet was preferred to the hand.

After four A.M. the fever began to lift. They checked and were relieved. Nelly put the kettle on for tea. At least this gave them the feeling that morning was well on its way. Outside the rain streamed down the windowpanes. Autumn had arrived. Feeling chilled from the lack of sleep, Ika went to fetch a cardigan from upstairs.

"Tell me about the winter garden," Nelly said after they had finished their tea.

It was like a leap back in time, and yet barely twenty-four hours had elapsed since she'd been working on it.

With her eyes shut, Ika began to describe it: "It's a covered garden, a sort of conservatory with glass walls and a glass roof. The door out of the lounge opens automatically when a person stands in front of it. So they can step *outside* while remaining inside. There's a path along the semicircular perimeter of the garden. On the left I picture a marshy area, and from it flows a waterfall that cascades through a stretch of stones down to a pond in the garden's center. A low clump of bamboo is also part of the design."

"I always thought bamboo was a tropical plant."

"There is tropical bamboo, of course. But there are also other varieties of bamboo that can handle lower temperatures. The winter garden's minimum temperature will be about seven degrees Celsius, so nothing will freeze.

"Will there be flowers, then?"

"Oh yes, more than you'd think."

"And what will it all look like in the summer?" Nelly wanted to know.

"It'll be beautiful, with delicate colors and lots of different shades of green. Nothing too lavish."

"But how do you keep the garden cool with the sun shining through a glass roof?"

"A sunshade will be installed on the inside that can be drawn along the roof as a kind of shield, and the semicircular front is almost entirely made of sliding panels that fit beside one another on rails. The circulation of the water through the garden will help maintain the low temperature as well."

"It all sounds lovely, Ika."

Mother was lying quietly, her eyes open now. Was she listening? Ika bent over her. Mother's eyes looked clear. The fever certainly appeared to have passed. Ika laid her hand on Mother's cheek. She was no longer so hot.

"Sounds just right for you," Mother said with a touch of reproach in her voice. "A winter garden. You used to charm the marguerites out of the ground."

"That was the *Doronicum*, Mother," said Nelly in the background.

Ika turned around in surprise. "Imagine you knowing that!"

"Abe," Nelly said.

"Is Abe coming?" asked Mother, then she indicated her wish to sit up straight against the pillows.

But as soon as Nelly attempted to lift her higher, Mother had to lie right back down again. Her eyes closed, and the clear-headedness faded, giving her face a strange expression. Then the eye sockets became blue and deeply sunken, and her mouth went slack and fell inwards. Ika and Nelly looked at each other sharing the same thought, yet they did not put it into words.

Mother's face was the face of a corpse—thin and colorless, with sunken features and the skin taut around the jaw. They both saw it and realized they shouldn't expect too much from the drop in her temperature.

The day's first light made the table lamp appear dim. It was Thursday, the 31st of October. At half past seven, they heard Willem at the back door. Nelly ran to the kitchen to meet him. Through the open door Ika saw their embrace.

"Did you sleep all right?" asked Nelly with her arms around Willem's neck.

"Yeah, I slept crossways. There was plenty of room," he boasted. But his hands, one on Nelly's neck and the other low on her back, spoke another language.

Ika turned away and heard their kiss. The sound reminded her of Mother's sucking, and this evoked similar feelings in her. It was an intimacy of which she had no experience. She was an outsider to such things. What did it feel like to rely on someone else's body as much as your own? What did it feel like when a child drank from you? Both these questions hurt in the same way. A pain deep within her. A shame that passed through to her arms and to her mouth, creating the strong desire to hold someone tight and to kiss that someone. Ika pulled the sliding doors shut behind her and walked over and sat on the bed. She sat for a long time with her mother's wrist in her hand, the pulse feeling weaker than before.

"Mother," Ika whispered, "why is there nobody for me? I mean, why can't I find anyone? And why am I so scared? How can I learn to love somebody . . . like Nelly has?"

Whether Mother heard Ika or not, there still would've been no response from her. Mother was too far away—too far to be called back.

"Mother, I'm late, but I still have things to ask you. I still have to know. You can't go yet. I need you."

The lump in her throat hurt, and a tear splashed onto Mother's arm. Ika stared at the single tear as it rolled slowly down the wrinkled skin and into the hollow of Mother's elbow. The drip innocently magnified a thin blue vein, a cord on the inside of the elbow. *What am I doing here?* she wondered. *Would it not have been better just to come to the funeral?*

Nelly entered the front room, holding two steaming cups in her hands, smelling of fresh coffee.

"Where's Willem?" Ika asked.

"At work. He only came to say that he got the wash started and to ask if I'd be able to hang it up later. He's great about housework," Nelly stated proudly.

Ika tried to get Mother to drink from the washcloth, but she didn't react. Nor did she react to Nelly's voice. Could it be that she was sleeping more and more deeply till possibly slipping into a coma? Nelly decided to stay and wait for Dr. Spaan to come as he had promised.

After he'd arrived and examined Mother, the doctor quickly tempered their enthusiasm over the fact that the fever had gone. "If she's still without the fever at five o'clock this afternoon, then you may become cautiously optimistic, but not before then," he said.

He then patted Mother on the cheek and called her name. Mother raised her eyes a little, pursing her lips as if to tell him that he was making too much noise. They had to laugh. It was so typical of Mother.

"Doctor . . ." Ika hesitated as he pulled on his trench coat in the hall, "is there still a chance. . . ? I mean, I still have to talk to her. I have to ask her something. So is it possible that she'll become lucid again . . . or not? How long will this stage last?"

Nelly came and stood beside her. "Yes, Doctor, what exactly do you expect to happen?"

Dr. Spaan looked from Ika to Nelly, then back to Ika and answered the last part of her question. "I expect this is indeed the end. She may go into a coma or she may hover on the edge. But her body cannot withstand much more. And if she's not drinking and not able to handle more medicine, I'm afraid nature will then take its course." He sighed. "It's a cruel illness," he said as he swung open the front door.

Raindrops began spattering onto the hall's granite floor. Dr. Spaan turned up his collar and walked swiftly toward the street. After he had banged the gate behind him, the doctor turned around and shouted the answer to the first part of Ika's question. "Don't expect too much. She's had a hard enough time."

Instantly, tears welled up in Ika's eyes, after which a suppressed anger nearly broke free. "Yes, but—" *What about me?* she had wanted to scream. *When do I get a chance?* But she didn't get any further than the first two words.

Dr. Spaan gave the gate a push that sent it shaking on its hinges. He then strode back to the front door. Ika had never seen before the expression of intense emotion that now spread across his face, a combination of pity and rage. He put out his hand and pulled Ika out into the rain.

In fear she wrapped both arms over her chest. What did he want?

He let go of her, and his voice was unexpectedly tender when he said, "Ika, if you stand in the rain all your life, you'll never get dry! Maybe you will. You're still young." With that the doctor pushed her back into the house and shut the door.

Ika bumped into Nelly, who let out a yell.

The bluish green of the hallway looked more than ever like a sea that threatened to pour in from above her.

✿

"Father, if you go in the rowboat, can we go with you?" Nelly had asked.

"I don't want any whining when I'm trying to fish," he'd said at first. But later they were allowed, because Mother had such a head-ache and had to be alone and lie down.

Nelly was four, and Ika nine. It was when Ika had resolved to be nice to everyone so they would in turn be nice to her. It had worked with Mr. Molenaar, though not with Father.

The day turned out to be a perfect one for fishing. And the two girls did their best to stay quiet. They knew if they annoyed their father they wouldn't be allowed to go out in the rowboat with him anymore.

During the afternoon, Nelly fell asleep in the bow of the boat, lying on Father's coat. Ika covered her with her own cardigan. Fa-ther caught nothing and he said nothing. Usually Ika was scared when out on the water, but that day the water was so shallow and smooth and calm that she began to enjoy it.

High in the air a few white clouds drifted by. The sky was a brilliant blue. *The color the sky should always be*, Ika thought.

And above it all, God lived. This was what Grandfather said. But how was that possible? Ika didn't know. Yet the blue suited God well, and the white was for the angels.

The water reflected the blue of the sky in a way that made it less threatening. Ika let her hand trail through the water, but Father soon told her to pull her hand out because she might scare away the fish. She had sighed deeply, something she never did when on the water, given how frightened she was of drowning. Even in the hall back at the house, she found she couldn't sigh deeply because of the bluish green coldness pressing in from all around her.

On this particular day, however, the thought of drowning seemed reduced merely to going to sleep, drifting away into nothingness.

"Father, does it hurt to drown?"

The boat rocked from the unexpected movement Father made as he turned around. "Don't start with the silly questions," he snapped.

His eyes looked angry and afraid at the same time. Ika had never seen him look so agitated.

Nelly woke up in confusion. She looked all around trying to regain her bearings.

"Ika, go and sit in the middle," ordered Father.

He sounded suddenly cross, yet nothing had happened. Surely they hadn't done anything wrong. Nelly moved over and sat in the middle too.

Rubbing her eyes, Nelly pouted and said, "You shouldn't be angry with us if we've been good." She looked like she was going to cry any second.

Father kept his eyes on his fishing rod. A few minutes later, since the fish weren't biting, he reeled in and started rowing for shore.

In her attempt to climb out of the boat, Ika's foot slipped on the pier's step. Immediately she felt Father's hand gripping the collar of her cardigan. He hoisted her up onto the pier, handling her roughly as though she had nearly fallen on purpose. She hadn't actually fallen because she was holding on tightly.

At home Mother was pacing the kitchen and holding a white washcloth against her forehead. This meant her headache was far from being finished. "Were they good girls?" she asked Father in her headache voice.

"I've no complaints," he replied, "but the oldest one isn't ever going again. She reminds me too much of you."

Ika looked from one face to the other and wondered how her attempt at being nice could have failed yet again. What had she done wrong?

Mother woke soon after Nelly had left for home. She drank a few sips of water, and then Ika changed the top sheet. Ika figured she'd wait to change the rest of the bedding when Nelly returned. She had to keep herself from constantly glancing over at the clock. Ika felt harassed, as if time were running out. Which in a way was precisely the situation. How much time would Nelly need to hang out the wash, to vacuum, and then do her shopping?

In desperation Ika sank down on the edge of the bed and took Mother's hand. "Mother . . ."

Mother looked slowly up at her, but it was hard for Ika to tell if she even recognized her.

"Mother, I'd like to know who my father was . . . or is." There, she'd said it, and in the silence that followed, Ika could hear her heart thumping.

Mother seemed to have heard the question, for Ika noticed her expression change. The change suggested Mother's defensiveness. The way she tightened her lips showed that, even if she were able, she had no desire to talk about Ika's biological father. Mother shut her eyes and turned her head away.

Then a wild urge came over Ika, and she seized Mother's shoulders. "Mother, tell me! Don't leave me here alone. I should know who my father is. What's the matter with you? Why could you never love me?" She shook the thin shoulders that offered no resistance. It was as if she were shaking a rag doll.

Mother must open her eyes; she must look at her. If for no other reason but to acknowledge that Ika existed. Ika screamed, and her voice seemed to tear away from her chest. "What, Mother? What could *I* do about it? If I shouldn't have come along, then why did you not kill me right away? You should *not* have allowed me to come into this world if you never had the intention or desire to love me."

The pain in Ika's chest became unbearable. Still, she pulled Mother up straight to force her to make eye contact. "Say it, Mother. Just say it at last. Far too much has gone wrong already. Don't do this to me. Don't die before I know why I was the outcast. I've always wanted to be like Nelly to you. Why couldn't you love me as you loved her?" Ika could scarcely get the words out, to wring them from her throat.

Mother's body swayed back and forth. She groaned as her eyes opened, large and helpless. Mother used to look at Grandfather the same way on Sunday mornings when they'd come home from church. She now held that same look, of someone called to account, of someone convicted of a crime.

Mother's mouth was trembling, so Ika let her go and the body flopped back into the pillows. At the same time Mother's head came into contact with the raised edge of the headboard. A new wave of sharp pain spread over her face. Her hands moved in the direction of her head but then stopped halfway and fell to her breast.

Wide-eyed, Mother stared up at Ika, as if a shutter had been raised above deep water. Unfathomable pools of stifling emptiness, loneliness, and remorse—what Ika had imagined hell to be like.

## CHAPTER SIXTEEN

TREMBLING, IKA JUMPED UP and stepped back toward the sliding doors. "What am I doing?" she said, her head against the stained glass. "What in heaven's name am I doing?" She thought of the kiss. It had been difficult to do, yet was so good. Had she now undone everything?

She had once crossed the threshold. She had grasped the idea that their relationship should all begin with her, that it would be a greater thing for her to forgive Mother than for Mother to admit her guilt. Had she come, then, to hear a confession or for reconciliation? Had her opportunity for forgiveness and reconciliation passed her by? Was it that God had given her a chance and she hadn't taken it?

She could hear Mother's voice calling for Nelly.

Ika went into the back room to find the Bible. She had to read the chapter from Isaiah. It wasn't in its usual place, but then she remembered that she'd taken it upstairs her first night there.

The hall surrounded her like chilly water. Ika raced up the stairs as she had done so many times in the past, stumbling and afraid.

She could still hear Mother's voice behind her, calling again for Nelly.

The stairs seemed three times longer than usual. In her rush to get to the bedroom, she struck her arm sharply against the doorjamb. Ignoring the pain, Ika scooped up the Bible, dropped onto the bed, and flipped the pages to Isaiah 43. The passage was there. Oh, thank God, it was still there. *Don't think about the past,* she said to herself. *God is making something new. Paths in the wilderness and streams in the desert. Now.*

She had to go back downstairs, to Mother. She stood up and straightened her back. She would read the passage out loud to Mother and resist the temptation to ask Mother more questions. Only say something more. Words that meant something to Mother—words of comfort. For Mother shouldn't drown in her own misery and guilt. She had to know what it said in Isaiah. "When thou passest through the waters, I will be with thee; and through the rivers, they shall not overflow thee."

In a few leaps Ika was downstairs. As she was about to enter the front room, the doorbell rang. She stood there indecisively. Who could it be? She hadn't the time for this, not for anyone else.

The bell rang again. Ika hurried to the door and, without opening it, shouted, "If it's urgent, come around the back, please!"

Not waiting for a response, she ran through the hall and into the front room. Mother lay there still, her eyes open. However they were so motionless and vacant looking that, for a moment, Ika feared Mother was no longer alive.

Lightly placing her fingers on Mother's neck, Ika felt for a pulse. A faint, irregular throb. Carefully she repositioned the pillows and Mother's head. She stroked the hair from Mother's face, smoothed the sheet. The little gestures were pledges. She would read to Mother about the new beginning and about the paths through the wilderness and about God who promised to go with her through the waters.

It was no longer difficult to kiss Mother or to caress her. Ika also found it easier to speak to her using names like Mummy, Mamma, and dear Mum.

Mother was crying now. Ika dabbed the tears away with the washcloth. Twice she put her index finger on Mother's lips when Mother tried to say something but couldn't produce any sound.

"Just rest now, Mother, and I'll read something for you. Try to relax and listen."

From a distance, there came the sound of footsteps outside the window, and later she heard the kitchen door swinging open. But the interruption didn't disturb her. It didn't matter. Ika's voice wavered, word by word, tasting the consolation in the meaning. Her eyes flitted back and forth from the page to Mother's face, to see whether the words were having any effect. Was Mother able to hear and understand?

After the first few lines, Ika stopped her reading because of getting the impression Mother was trying to say something.

"Once more." The two words had come like a sigh from Mother's mouth.

So Ika started over. " 'But now thus saith the Lord that created thee, O Jacob, and he that formed thee, O Israel, Fear not: for I have redeemed thee, I have called thee by thy name; thou art mine. When thou passest through the waters, I will be with thee. . . .' "

She clasped Mother's hand, which was moving aimlessly over the sheet. " 'Since thou wast precious in my sight, thou hast been honourable, and I have loved thee: therefore will I give men for thee, and people for thy life. Fear not: for I am with thee: I will bring thy seed from the east—' "

Someone walked through the back room, treading heavily. The panes in the sliding doors rattled, giving Ika the idea it was a purposeful step. Then the doors were slid fully open with a single but forceful action.

Simone's anxious brown eyes encouraged a smile to creep over Ika's face. She stepped into the room and sat down in the chair in the corner. The chair creaked in protest. Simone didn't say anything, but clearly indicated that Ika should continue with her reading. And so Ika looked down again at the Bible on her lap.

After she had put down the receiver, Ika thought that the voice could just as easily have belonged to a man as to a woman. She had been invited for an interview with Berger's Landscape Gardening.

The following afternoon she was shown into a small office. It was new and still smelled of paint. There was a small reception area, which must have been the showpiece. Fresh green foliage plants of many different varieties had been artistically arranged around a small aviary. But Ika didn't see any birds. Inside the aviary had been set a shallow water basin, expertly fashioned, depicting a relief of a beach with real shells. The basin reminded Ika of her dove at home, for the dove loved to splash around in the water.

One of the three doors opened and was then banged shut behind a furious young man. Appalled, Ika looked on as he brushed past her legs with long strides while rubbing his forehead.

At the exit he spun around and said to Ika, "That woman's a she-devil, an absolute fathead! What's a person like that doing in this business?"

Ika realized he was talking about the female boss of Berger's. He obviously wasn't very pleased with the way his interview had gone.

Ika shifted her attention to the door that would soon be opening for her. From behind the closed door she heard a metallic clank, and although she didn't know it at the time, it was the first of many occasions when Ika would hear Simone kicking the filing cabinet.

When the door finally opened, Ika jumped to her feet and took a few steps forward but then abruptly halted. The woman standing in the doorway was large and sturdy. Yes, Ika had expected someone like this. She proceeded on and held out her right hand.

The woman shook Ika's hand firmly while looking at her with searching brown eyes. "Do you have any problems with working for a woman?"

Ika shook her head. Why should she?

The woman walked behind Ika so as to close the door behind them. Her sharp angry movements caused a small hurricane in the room, as the papers on the desk were sent flying to the floor. Ika crouched down to gather them together.

"What about working for a *she-devil*?" the angry voice above her inquired.

A deep blush crept up Ika's neck, as if she'd been caught eavesdropping.

With the woman's next movement, the papers got scattered around the room again in a flurry. She removed something from the filing cabinet and, still showing her vexation, shut the lower drawer with an impressive kick.

*The noise I heard earlier,* Ika thought. "You could easily break your toe doing that." The words were out before Ika could stop them. She shocked herself and clapped her hand over her mouth.

"Then maybe one day I'll have to get an artificial foot," the woman said, limping back to her chair. She laid out the papers on her desk.

Ika looked at her uncertainly, tinged with an underlying amusement.

"Call me Simone," she said. "Now, what sort of birds do you think are coming into the aviary?"

Instantly Ika answered, "Turtledoves."

And this was the beginning of their friendship.

Now in the front room, Simone sat behind Ika on the brown velvet chair, the arms of which disappeared under her bulk. Ika glanced up once more before reading on. Simone gave her a don't-mind-me look, and a warm feeling, which nearly got her crying, passed through Ika's chest.

She decided to back up a bit and repeat the words from before. " 'But now thus saith the Lord that created thee, O Jacob, and he that formed thee, O Israel, Fear not: for I have redeemed thee, I have called thee by thy name; thou art mine. When thou passest through the waters, I will be with thee. . . .' " Then Ika skipped down a few verses and reread, " 'Since thou wast precious in my sight, thou hast been honourable, and I have loved thee: therefore will I give men for thee, and people for thy life. Fear not: for I am with thee. . . .' "

Putting down the Bible, Ika looked solemnly at Mother. Mother's eyes had become restful, her breathing peaceful as if sleeping. She had hardly noticed Simone's arrival. She lay there still and full of submission, teetering on that border between existence and nonexistence, where thought had receded a far distance away.

The quiet breathing was all her body could still do. Everything was concentrated on this. Everything waited for the next meager inhalation of air and hoped it would be there.

Ika turned her chair a little toward Simone. With the first of tears tracing their way down her cheeks, she said, "I've done some terrible things, Simone. I've hurt her. I've shaken her."

All at once she was sitting with her head on Simone's knee and letting go of all the tears she'd bottled up over the last days. Simone put her hand on the shaking back and stroked it awkwardly, but in a heartfelt way. Ika could tell Simone was tense, for she smelled a mixture of soap and sweat, the way she always smelled when in an uncomfortable situation. Simone was here.

"What made you decide to come?" asked Ika, when later they were sitting together at the table in the back room.

Simone shrugged.

It was strange how well Simone fit in—as if she'd always been there. As if each day she had been sitting there at the table, her bosom resting on its surface, while flattening the tablecloth with her elbows. She looked through the geraniums and into the garden. Without hesitation she had named all the plants.

"I was headed to the bonsai exhibition. You know, the one we got the tickets for. I was making really good time and then I saw the turnoff to here. Before I'd even thought where to go, I found your street. So I figured I'd stop in and see how things were going."

It was as simple as that. Simone just wanted to see how things were going. Ika stood up and went over to Mother. She lay motionless except for her breathing, which at the moment was light and superficial and made the sheet move up and down.

Ika stroked her warm, dry cheek. Mother's eyes flew open as if she'd been shocked, then immediately closed again. Ika discovered that she could give her a kiss spontaneously. The parting had begun. She could feel it in herself. "Mother, I'm here. You know, I'm staying."

In the back room, Simone had found the drawing of the winter garden. She made approving noises and scratched her neck.

Ika smiled at the familiar gesture. After she made coffee, she came and stood beside Simone and showed her what she had done, also explaining what she'd not yet put on paper. Simone nodded and filled in the gaps, leaning on the table so heavily that it tilted on just two legs.

It was a strained good-bye, especially for Simone who tended to avoid intimacy. "I'm so pleased that you came," Ika said. "It was good to see you."

Simone clapped Ika's back in a way that was restrained for her, though was still quite hard. Ika gave a gulp, which gave Simone reason enough to continue with more clapping. Suddenly there was a sort of quick hug.

Ika had felt Simone's thick arms around her back and heard her say, "All right, I'm off then. Don't let yourself get boxed in here. Oh, sorry, that wasn't a nice remark." Simone let go, a little dismayed.

Weighted down with her shopping, Nelly walked in just as Simone was leaving. Nelly was standing in the doorway, looking in amazement at Ika and Simone. Ika introduced them to each other, then walked with Simone to her car.

"Don't get too involved with the bonsai," Ika warned through the open car window. "I don't like things that have to be clipped and pruned and kept small to make them beautiful."

"You shouldn't get too personally involved in anything," Simone replied as she started the car.

As she was busy unloading groceries from her bag onto the kitchen counter, Nelly said, "What a fatty," referring to Simone. It didn't sound all that contemptuous but more like she was stating a mere fact. Still, Ika thought it a nasty remark.

"She's the best friend I've got," Ika said, but Nelly had her back toward her.

"I was rushed off my feet and still had to go to the post office, and there was a long line in front of me," Nelly said, breathing hard.

"I've made some coffee. Pour yourself a cup while I finish clearing this up," said Ika. Suddenly she got the feeling that perhaps Nelly's life wasn't as easy as she had imagined.

Later they stood at Mother's bedside wondering what they should do next. Every now and then, Mother would slowly open her eyes and struggle to focus only to close them again with a frown. It would be hours before afternoon, when Dr. Spaan was scheduled to arrive.

"She should be washed," Ika said. "This morning I only washed her face and changed the top sheet."

Nelly nodded and pulled the sheet back. A ring of moisture had stained the bottom sheet, and they could both smell something sweetish.

"She's wet the bed," Nelly whispered, sounding shocked. "Now she'll *have* to be washed. At first I thought it might be better to wait till the nurse comes tomorrow, but now . . ."

It was horrible to see Mother lying in a wet bed. It wasn't like her. But on the other hand, Ika felt that Mother shouldn't be disturbed, that it was a kind of sacrilege to startle this dying body with soap and water and scrubbing. Ika threw her arm around Nelly's shoulder as though trying to protect her in advance from what she was about to say. "Just wait, Nelly. We'll wash her later when it's all over. That's better, I think. We can't do it now. She looks so peaceful." Ika felt the tension shooting into Nelly's back.

"Do you think this is the end?" Nelly asked hesitantly, her eyes filling up.

Ika nodded.

"You're wrong, Ika." But a long look at Mother's face convinced her that what Ika had said was indeed the truth. The tension drained from Nelly's shoulders and, looking for support now that grief had taken possession of her, she hid her face in Ika's neck without saying a word.

When they were children, Nelly had cried with Ika about her sad times, such as when she had been punished, deserved or not, just as she was doing now. Finally, her whole body communicated a feeling of resignation, clearer than saying aloud, "That's how it's going to be."

After a trembling sigh, Nelly lifted her head from Ika's shoulder and, with eyes full of sadness, said, "If only I knew she'd been happy, then it would be less difficult. Were you able to talk to her? Has she told you anything yet? Oh, Ika, you'll never find out afterward."

Ika made a helpless gesture with her hands. "I've certainly tried to talk to her. Earlier when you were away, before Simone came." While she was speaking, a blush crept over her face. "No, she told me nothing. I . . . At first I was angry with her and then I was nasty to her. But then I thought about that passage in Isaiah that has helped me so much, and so I read it to her." Ika's words made what happened with Mother seem insignificant, so she added, "I'll look it up for you later."

Nelly nodded, repeating the last word, "Later . . ."

They both knew what this meant. *Later*, as in after Mother's death.

"I think it's awful that she's lying in a wet bed. Surely we could take away the wet sheet and clean her," Nelly said.

Ika nodded, went to the linen closet, and took out a clean sheet. Carefully Nelly lifted Mother, while Ika changed the sheet under her. She listened as Nelly spoke soft soothing words to Mother.

Mother opened her eyes, looking up at Nelly. "I don't feel good, Nelly," she said rather lucidly. Then she seemed to sink away, unresponsive now to their voices.

Now that it was coming down to the end, they both felt increasingly afraid and unsure. They decided to call Dr. Spaan.

The doctor was quick to arrive. He shook his head when he first beheld Mother. "Do you want your children to say good-bye?

Have you phoned your husband yet?" he asked Nelly.

Nelly brought her hand up to her throat, looking incapable of giving an answer.

Ika interjected and said the words Nelly didn't want to say. "So this is the end?"

Dr. Spaan only nodded. Then turning to Mother and taking her hand, he whispered, "Her fighting spirit has left, and her body doesn't want to go on anymore." He pulled back the blankets and carefully examined the emaciated body. As he straightened his back, he continued, "There's a lot of fluid forming in her lungs now. She'll get short of breath and eventually drown or suffocate in the fluid that has accumulated. Do you still want her to stay at home?" The doctor paused, then added, "She'll hardly notice anything at all about the hospital, as long as your faces are around in case she gets a clear moment."

Nelly and Ika only needed to look at each other to know that neither of them wanted Mother to go to the hospital. "No, we'll keep her here . . . to die at home," Nelly whispered, and Ika nodded in agreement.

Dr. Spaan reached over and squeezed Nelly's hand and then Ika's shoulder.

*It feels as though we're deciding right here and now that Mother should die*, thought Ika. With heavy feet, she walked behind the doctor and Nelly to the back room, and there the doctor gave them instructions on what to do should Mother become short of breath.

Ika saw how Nelly was listening attentively, with her head a little to one side.

*No, surely not a decision about Mother's death,* she told herself, *but rather an acceptance of it.*

## CHAPTER SEVENTEEN

DURING THE AFTERNOON Willem and the boys came by.
The two boys walked timidly through the kitchen. Willem wiped
his forehead. He'd had a terrible rush to get there.

The younger boy, Dirk-Willem, looked the most like Nelly. Ika
was shocked by the resemblance and found it hard to take her eyes
off him, for he reminded her so much of Nelly when she first went
to school. At that time Ika had to protect her, and now she automatically felt an urge to protect Dirk-Willem too.

Dirk-Willem clung to his mother, as he looked anxious and shy
in the oppressive atmosphere. Nelly caressed his girlish blond curls.
With his large blue eyes and innocent expression, he looked like a
miniature angel.

Ika then remembered what Nelly had said about him: "He's a
wriggler, the little monkey!" But looking as he did now, Ika couldn't
imagine him acting naughty in any way.

She could imagine this of Abe, however, though now he was
also behaving rather bashfully. Abe had more spirit, more fire in his
eyes. She could see he'd just had a shower, as the water droplets still
glistened on the spikes of his hair.

Ika noticed that Nelly was much more independent without Willem around, but this was only because Willem exuded so much strength. In a quiet voice Nelly told the boys what the doctor had said, how Mother was going downhill rapidly.

"Is she going to die? I mean . . . this very day?" stuttered Abe.

Willem put his hand on Abe's shoulder. "It's very likely. She's getting weaker and weaker, and there comes a point where the body can't go on, when everything stops."

Dirk-Willem removed his thumb from his mouth long enough to ask, "Will she ever be alive again?" Nelly lifted him onto her knee, but he immediately jumped off again. "I'm a big boy now!" he said loudly, then licked away the dribble of saliva running down his wrist and wiped his thumb on his shirt.

Abe provided the answer Dirk-Willem was looking for. "When you die, you can't be alive again—that's it. She'll either go to heaven or to hell." He turned to Ika. "Auntie Ika, do you believe that God lets people go to hell? I wouldn't like to live in heaven with a God like that. Anyway, I'd like to see first if heaven even exists. Space travel hasn't yet—"

Willem pulled at Abe's arm. "Hey, Abe, let's talk about space travel some other time. We're here for Grandma, remember?" He jerked his head in the direction of the sliding doors.

Abe's mouth clamped shut and he bowed his head.

"Come on," Willem said, pushing the sliding doors wider open. Now Dirk-Willem wanted to be carried, and Nelly hid behind Willem's strength. Abe followed reluctantly, with Ika close behind, her hand resting lightly on his shoulder.

Abe looked up at her. "Do you think Granny was a good person?" The question reverberated over and over in Ika's head. The room seemed to spin, yet Abe's darkened eyes remained fastened on her. "Do you think Granny was a good person?" he had asked. The question had shifted the standard from God to Mother.

The shooting pain began again behind her ribs. Ika pushed her fist against her breastbone to control it. She swallowed hard, and the hand that before had touched Abe's shoulder so lightly now suddenly pressed down, grasping for support.

"Do you think that God loves Granny?" was his next question.

Ika nodded, for she couldn't make herself speak.

Yes, of course God loves Mother. After all, He'd know all the reasons behind the chilly coldness that she had breathed in and out almost her entire life. He'd know about the winter garden in Mother's heart, about the uncultivated soil at the bottom of Mother's soul, about her sunless life.

Suddenly Ika sensed what it might be like to walk through her own winter garden. The place was cool, yet not unpleasantly so. Around her head blew a soft breeze, a springlike wind that swayed the grasses and brought everything to life. The fountain sprayed forth its droplets far and wide, and the plantation of bamboos rustled in the background. Yes, there had to be wind in the winter garden. The wind is spirit, a sign of life.

Mother opened her eyes with surprise. Had the wind touched her too?

Abe's shoulder twitched in shock. He took a step forward, kneeled, and gathered up his grandmother's hand. "It's me, Granny . . . Abe. Do you still know me?"

For a brief moment Mother looked as if struggling to smile, but then the eyelids fell shut again.

"Granny, do you still know me?" echoed Dirk-Willem.

Willem, who had been standing behind the two boys, stepped forward and said, "Give Grandma a kiss and say good-bye. Maybe she won't hear it, but she'll feel it all the same."

"Granny," Abe said, "We're all here."

His innocent gaze traveled around the whole group of them and then came to rest once more on the quiet gray face amid the pillows.

"We're all here" is what Mr. Molenaar had said when the principal was buried. They stood there in the cemetery in their funeral clothes. A cold, drizzly rain studded their dark coats with bright pearls. Mr. Molenaar was the last to speak, just after Grandfather, who had spoken about the shortness of life, and the chairman of the school board, who spoke of the empty place that had now arisen.

Only the soft voice of Mr. Molenaar could be heard above the shuffling and the coughing. Not many were paying attention any longer. People had heard enough and wanted to have their coffee. Perhaps there would be a roll as well.

But Ika pricked up her ears, because her teacher always talked so nicely. He spoke as if the dead principal could still hear.

"We're all here. Here, to think of you in gratitude. We were all very shocked that you left us so suddenly. But we believe that you were expected in the Father's house, and that you have now gone to your eternal home."

Now the teacher's voice sounded even softer. After all, he was talking about heaven. And he never talked about heaven without being moved, though he'd kept himself from weeping. Which was good, because so many people were crying already. The principal's wife seemed out of control, and her sisters nearby cried just as loudly.

On their way back to the church, along the narrow path that ran between the tombstones, Ika heard different people grumbling. They complained that it was a shame the schoolchildren had been allowed to stand at the front, that the minister—Grandfather—had preached for so long, and that the chairman of the school board was always getting lost in what he said and so repeated himself. They also talked about Mr. Molenaar, who, they said, had taken the whole thing far too lightly. For if the minister himself didn't dare give them any clear assurance regarding the principal being safe in heaven, then what right had Mr. Molenaar to talk about such a thing as if fact? Therefore, it was "unspeakable" that a person such as Mr. Molenaar should be teaching at the school.

Later on, as Ika was walking with her class back to the school building, she slid her hand into Mr. Molenaar's and asked, "Do you think the principal heard what you said?"

Mr. Molenaar smiled and turned the question back on her. Ika just shrugged her shoulders. He then pulled a handkerchief from his pocket and blew his nose, snorting as usual.

Ika could barely understand him, as he began talking from behind his handkerchief. He had said something about if God thought it necessary for the principal to hear things from Earth, then He would've made it possible for him to hear. He went on to say that it was good for those at the funeral to be reminded that we were there, because we would all find it hard to go on without him.

"But didn't Grandfather mean that too?" Ika had to ask.

The teacher squeezed her hand. "Maybe, but then people should say what they mean."

She squeezed his hand back, for that was quite clear to her.

"We're all here," Abe had said.

The clock's ticking pierced the silence.

While Nelly drove the boys to her in-laws, Willem stepped outside for a smoke and started pacing the garden path. Ika could hear him returning each time toward the back window, the gritty sound of sand between his shoes and the paving stones. It was much easier to focus on this sound than the sound of Mother's breathing.

With each hour that had passed, her breaths came with greater irregularity. Ika got short of breath just listening to it. She waited tensely until Mother's bottom lip quivered again, until she sucked in a tiny bit more oxygen. Sometimes Willem had passed under the window twice before the lip would quiver again.

From far away came the faint throbbing sound of an airplane. As time went on, the plane, or planes now, seemed to be getting closer, for the noise had grown louder and more distinct. Willem tapped on the back window and pointed, causing Ika to look up. He indicated that she should come outside.

"It must be a training exercise from that military base nearby. Come and take a look. There are seven of them," he shouted enthusiastically.

Ika took a few steps toward joining Willem, but a movement from Mother made her return to the bed. *Maybe the noise woke her up*, Ika thought. Suddenly Mother's eyes came open. She reached out her hands as if wanting to be lifted up.

Ika used both her hands to pull Mother toward herself. Sitting together on the side of the bed, Ika could feel that Mother's body was trying to nestle up to her. It was such a feeble and helpless attempt, however, that Ika felt compelled to wrap her arms tightly around her mother's narrow back and remain completely still till the thundering rumble of the airplanes had passed over.

The panes of the sliding doors rattled violently as though wanting out of their frames. She heard Willem screaming something, and then the room was so full of the noise of the airplanes' engines that Ika involuntarily clasped Mother even more firmly. Just when the planes were flying low over the house, the vibrations increased to such a level that the closet door flew open and a pile of Mother's underclothes toppled onto the floor. Then from the back room came the sound of breaking glass, as the dove flapped anxiously against the side of the cage.

Mother's head sank onto Ika's arm. Ika placed her cheek against the thin gray hair. The smell of illness and unwashed hair crept into her nostrils as she breathed in. It was as if she were inhaling Mother, as if Mother were being deflated in her arms, growing smaller and smaller all the time.

Finally the sound rolled away into the distance, leaving in its wake everything in an improbable silence. The only movement was that of her own chest as she breathed. Ika could also feel the blood pulsing in her neck. *How strange to be so conscious of this now*, she thought. As if this were the only difference between them, now as they sat so rigidly together, entangled with each other.

She waited for a moment. She knew that when she laid Mother down onto the pillows, it would be for the very last time. Ika couldn't explain the reason why, but now that Mother lay against her so lifeless, she was dearer and softer than ever.

" 'I have called thee by thy name; thou art mine.' "

The words came of their own accord. God would have to receive Mother now.

Willem grumbled in the back room as he carefully picked up

the splinters of glass. How quiet it was now after the thundering racket of the airplanes.

When Ika breathed out, Mother's hair moved. And with the slight movement, it felt as though Mother slipped away from her arms.

The sliding doors clattered open and there stood Willem holding in his hands the photos of Father and Grandfather and their frames. The glass was all shattered, and the frames had come apart.

Immediately Willem noticed how Ika and Mother were sitting together in a kind of open-ended silence, interrupted a moment later by the dove's call. Whether in shock or relief, the bird called at least seven times.

Nelly's eyes showed her panic when she rushed into the room. With a shriek, she fell on her knees beside the bed and grasped Mother's hands, which Ika had gently positioned on the edge of the clean sheet.

Whimpering slightly, Nelly stroked her mother's hands. "How could you not have waited, Mother? I can't believe I wasn't here when the time came." She turned to Willem and Ika with an infuriated look on her face. "You shouldn't have let me go! It's not fair. All these months I looked after her, and then at the end, I wasn't here. Why did you not hold me back? Why did you not think to take the boys away yourself?"

Willem approached her, knelt down, and put his arm around her. "But, Nelly, we didn't know. We didn't know it would happen just now. And it was you who suggested that you take the boys."

He helped her stand up, but because he wasn't prepared for her launching herself against him in her upset state, he staggered a little. Then like a child he led her into the back room. Ika could hear Willem's quiet voice talking in between Nelly's hysterical sobbing. Ika smiled above Mother's face, which had become whiter already. Willem, her brother-in-law, was worth his weight in gold.

As Dr. Spaan was walking up the garden path, Ika hurried to get to the door before him. *He shouldn't ring the bell now*, she thought.

In the dim hallway he looked at her with searching eyes. Ika smiled.

"How are you?" he asked with his heavy voice.

She nodded and smiled again, for she couldn't speak. Her voice had left her. Instead, she motioned with her hand while holding open the door for him.

Dr. Spaan stood for a long time by the bed. His big hands hung aimlessly from his arms, which seemed longer than usual. When he turned and pushed open the sliding doors with considerable force, Ika was surprised how he cursed.

A few moments later, Ika and Nelly and Dr. Spaan sat together at the kitchen table. The doctor stirred his coffee while writing down in illegible strokes the telephone number of the undertaker to call. He knew it by heart. "Do you want to prepare your mother yourselves," he asked, "or should someone else come and do it?"

Knowing the usual way these things were done, Nelly hastened to say she'd do it herself. Then looking suddenly shocked, she said, "I must fetch the boys! They don't know yet." In her haste to stand up, she knocked over her cup. The coffee spread over the plush tablecloth. "Oh, this tablecloth was Mother's pride and joy," said Nelly, immediately clapping her hand to her mouth.

Was Mother's pride and joy. In the past tense. It came home for Ika while she was rinsing out the tablecloth. The coffee mixed with the tap water that flowed and flowed, and the brown stains fanned out thinner and thinner into the granite sink.

Life was like that, becoming thinner and thinner till finally being taken away in a stream from many sources. Mother had died. There was nothing more.

Nelly was crying with big childish sobs. Only with the greatest difficulty had Willem managed to persuade her not to go and tell the boys so soon before nighttime.

"Dirk-Willem will be in bed already. Honestly, tomorrow will be soon enough. Nothing's going to change now. Later this evening, when Abe is in bed, I'll walk over to my parents. Try to calm down, Nelly. You're getting yourself all worked up."

Dr. Spaan patted Nelly on the back and promised to give her something to help her sleep. "Nonsense, it's no extra trouble," he said to Ika who was getting his coat for him.

As he left the house, Ika peered through the green pane of the front door. From the back he didn't look so old. Still, he was at least ten years older than Mother. Ten years, and perhaps he'd live another twenty years yet. Mother was fifty-three, a very young age to die.

Was this why the doctor had cursed earlier—because he couldn't do anything to help Mother? Because he couldn't win against the disease? It wasn't like Dr. Spaan, although he was known to be a rough-spoken man on occasion. But cursing didn't suit him.

Ika lingered in the hallway for a while, where a strange silence hung in the air. After the deafening roar of the airplanes, the silence seemed now to stick to all the little things: to the coats draped on the hallstand, the worn-out runner on the stairs, the sheets on the drying rack in the stairwell. Everything appeared so motionless, so rigid.

The only sound came from Nelly in the other room. When she was upset she sounded like a child. Even the soft, faltering conversation didn't lift the silence, but rather made it heavier and deeper. Or did it just seem this way because of the twilight spreading over the hall?

The clock struck seven. Willem stretched out, yawning loudly, causing the wicker chair to creak in unison.

She would have to go in. What was she doing staying out in the cold hall so long? The last of the light could be seen as it crept along the walls of the hallway. Green light.

## CHAPTER EIGHTEEN

MOTHER HAD MADE A WILL.

Ika sat looking stunned, the envelope in her hand. It was something that had come completely unexpected—for Mother to have a will drawn up.

She turned the paper over and over in her hand. It was Mother's handwriting all right. Written in beautifully perfect flourishes were Mother's maiden name and the instruction, *To be opened after my death.*

Nelly knew about the will. Mother had told her when she had first learned of the cancer: "It doesn't need to be official, like through a lawyer. What I have to say isn't that important. But still, Nelly, you need to know that it's there, in the top drawer of the dresser."

When Willem had called the undertaker, Nelly thought back to Mother's words. She then went and removed the drawer from the dresser and set it on the table in front of Ika.

There were many things to sift through, such as swimming diplomas, old school report cards, the birth announcements of Abe and Dirk-Willem. The drawer was crammed full, which made Ika push it to the middle of the table but not before she'd removed the brown envelope that lay on top.

She looked over at Nelly who waited expectantly, leaning against a chair. Nelly was curious and so she motioned for Ika to open it. Ika couldn't help noticing Nelly's eyes and how intently they were fixed on the envelope. It was strange what curiosity did to people. Up until now, Nelly had been inconsolable. What was she expecting from the letter?

"Couldn't we wait till tomorrow?" Ika said tentatively. She suddenly longed for the serenity of her flat, for her own little kitchen where she loved to read the newspaper with her back to the radiator.

Nelly shook her head. "Maybe there's something in it about the funeral, and who knows but the funeral insurance policy may be there as well. We've got to know before the man from the undertaker's comes."

Ika pushed the envelope across to Nelly.

"Go ahead and open it," said Nelly impatiently. "Don't you think your history may very well be in there too?"

"No," Ika said, "Mother wasn't like that. If she would not say it, then she wouldn't write it down either."

Although Ika used a sharp knife to open the envelope, it left an untidy raveled edge behind, as if the brown paper resisted being opened.

There were two folded sheets of paper from a lined pad inside.

Ika unfolded them. The first was a list of addresses for the mourning cards. The second began with *Dear Nelly*. It wasn't a long letter. The writing stopped just before the fold in the middle. Ika handed the paper to Nelly who held it under the light.

> *Dear Nelly,*
>
> *When I'm gone, please bring the dove to my eldest daughter. Take her the red coral necklace from my mother as well. You know, the one with the gold catch. It's behind the new hand towels in the linen closet. Don't forget to tell her that Mr. Molenaar has asked about her many a time. He's been living for years in the old vineyard.*
>
> 

*Your Mother*
*19th July*

Shocked, Nelly stared at the paper. She clutched at the envelope, but it was empty. Apart from the addresses, there was no other writing on the first sheet. After collapsing onto a chair, Nelly tossed the letter back on the table, into the beam of the lamp. The writing stood out boldly against the white of the paper. "Not a word for me," she said with a tremor in her voice. "Not a word for the boys. No greeting. No thanks. Nothing." Nelly picked up the letter again, reading the first sentence once more aloud. "Why does she say that so oddly? 'Please bring the dove to my eldest daughter.' What sort of stupid will is this? You'd think I didn't exist at all."

Willem, who had joined them earlier when Nelly was first reading the will, now scooped up the letter and folded it in half. "Now,

Nell, there's no need to be jealous. You saw your mother every day."

The flashing dots of light behind Ika's eyes were a bad sign. Tomorrow she wouldn't be worth much. She wanted to go home to her own bed right away. The low attic roof of the bedroom she'd been staying in had become claustrophobic. Ika stood up and went through the kitchen toward the back door.

"Where are you going?" asked Nelly to Ika's back as she walked away.

"Only to get a breath of fresh air," she said, reaching for the doorknob.

The backyard was still wet from the recent rain, but now the clouds had disappeared and a thin moon hung in the sky. Ika walked along, choosing her steps carefully along the garden path. The cold dropped down on her and crept up her legs. If it stayed as clear as it was now, everything would certainly freeze during the night. Tomorrow would be the first of November, All Saints' Day.

*My eldest daughter. Why not Ika, or Ikabod?* she wondered. When Ika came to the little gate at the back and put her hands on the cold, wet wood, she remembered that there was something mentioned about Mr. Molenaar. So he *was* still alive, and Mother wanted her to know it. However scant Mother's will was, it was important nonetheless.

Mr. Molenaar. Through the glistening darkness of the wet street, Ika could still see his face as he talked in front of the class so long ago. His hands and his mouth brought to life the stories he used to tell. And the wrinkles around his eyes, even the badly shaved, pockmarked cheeks. *Don't forget to tell her that Mr. Molenaar has asked about her many a time.* Ika felt as though she'd changed on the spot back into the child from his class.

❧

The red coral necklace was lying on the table when Ika returned. She shivered, as the cold had bitten through her clothing and through her hair.

"There it is," said Nelly.

"I don't need it, Nelly. You take it and enjoy it, if you want. Really."

Willem's eyes turned angry, Nelly's more sullen.

Their reactions surprised Ika and she almost had to smile. She picked up the heavy string of beads. Grandmother had always worn them. She had inherited the necklace, too, from someone on her mother's side—wealthy folks from Zeeland. Ika let the necklace slip onto Nelly's knee. "Please take it, Nelly. It's Mother's only piece of jewelry. You have much more right to it than I have. Anyway, I'd never wear it. Just like Mother hardly ever wore it."

"I always thought it was beautiful," Nelly said as her fingers fondled the beads.

Willem jumped up from his slumped position. "If you take it, Nell, I will personally flush the thing down the toilet. What's all this about? You're acting like a little child here?"

Nelly jerked back her hand, and the necklace fell to the floor. Willem snatched it up and stuck it in the front pocket of his pants and then glowered at his wife.

"Everything's all right. I didn't say that I . . ." Nelly grumbled.

Ika looked over the address list, counting how many cards they would need, while Willem answered the knock at the front door. It would be the undertaker. Willem greeted him, took his coat, and showed him inside.

Ika knew the man well. Jan Jonker was his name. He was only a few years older than she and had begun to look like the image of his father. His hands looked cracked from dryness. Shaking one of them reminded her of a mummy.

Suddenly an idea about the winter garden shot through her head. She'd work that evening, while the idea was still fresh. For she knew now how she wanted it.

Over the muted conversation about the coffin and the funeral service arrangements, Ika could see the rustling bamboo and hear the splashing fountain. The effect of a soft wind could be produced using a fan, to blow the warmer air from the left wall along the windows. This would also work to combat condensation on the glass. There should be something with moss in it arranged near the pool.

The voice whined on, recommending various types of mourning cards.

Ika only listened to the tone, ignoring the individual words. She didn't see the point of getting handmade paper, nor could she understand the significance of a silver-gray edge versus just a gray edge for the cards.

When Ika pushed back her chair to stand up, Nelly said cattily, "Are you going to walk away, then?"

Ika noticed that Willem was also rather upset as he said in a similar tone, "You've got the necklace already." The hint of a laugh appeared in his angry eyes when they met Ika's.

Nelly continued looking through the book of samples, a bright red flush creeping up from her neck.

"Could I have been in the same class as you at school?" Jan Jonker asked Ika directly.

"If so, then you must've been held back a few years," Ika replied. She didn't care anymore. She had to leave, up to her little room. She couldn't stand it any longer, all the drivel and the depressing talk at the table.

In the hallway she closed her eyes and went blindly up the stairs. She didn't need a light; she knew the house by feel. When she reached the top of the stairs, she stopped. Nelly was crying again.

Ika let herself fall onto the bed. The bed's mattress sprang up and down under her weight. The streetlight in front of the house shed its light directly on the picture hanging on the wall. From where she lay, she could read the words inscribed near the picture's bottom: "Suffer the little children to come unto me, and forbid them not, for of such is the kingdom of God."

She gazed at the different children's faces, looking to find some of Mother's features, yet she did not see any. It was strange that she could see Nelly again and again in almost every child's face.

She shouldn't have been so rude to the undertaker downstairs. He hadn't meant any harm with his question. Ika could hear Willem seeing him out. What was Jan still muttering about in the cold hallway? Willem didn't say much back. Then came the bang of the door, which seemed to shake the whole front of the house—hardly the thing to do in a recently bereaved household.

Ika could hear footsteps on the stairs, probably Nelly. Why did she suddenly feel like locking the door? She mustn't act like a child. But everybody worked through their grief in different ways. Was she grieving? Was Nelly grieving? Was Mother somebody to be grieved over? Nelly would certainly miss Mother. Mother was part of Nelly's life, whether this was a positive or a negative factor.

It seemed like such a long time since she'd been home. Getting up and going to work, opening the curtains in the morning and enjoying the view over the park, making sandwiches for lunch later, locking the door and going downstairs, talking to Simone about a project, making out schedules for the boys. And in the evenings, there was the silence of her own room, the sighing of the heating system, or sometimes the banging of doors in the flat above.

Nelly knocked. This touched Ika, feeling like a punishment. "Come in!" she called.

Nelly pushed her way into the room. "Are you lying here in the dark and cold?" Nelly sat on the edge of the bed. It seemed they did nothing else these days other than to sit on the edges of beds. "Ika, I've been a stupid fool." Nelly's voice sounded chastened. She didn't see Ika smile. "I should not have gone on about the necklace. It doesn't matter. Please take it and forget what I said."

Ika felt Nelly laying the necklace on her stomach. She could feel the weight of it and its coldness through her blouse. She moved, and the necklace slid beside her onto the blanket.

Nelly took this as a refusal. She sighed and began to falter again.

Ika sat up and put her arms around her. "Stop talking about it, girl, and give the thing to Willem. His idea to flush it wasn't so bad after all. I don't want anything to come between us. We were only just starting again." The words couldn't say it all, but the gesture did.

Nelly sniffed a little and rubbed her nose. Ika gave her a handkerchief. Nelly made a few blowing noises and peered out over the handkerchief and then at last began to laugh.

"We're being silly," Ika said, standing up.

Smothered in the hankie, Nelly replied, "Do you think so? I feel so strange, as if I was almost glad it's all over. Yet I'm angry too. They are the wrong sort of feelings. I can't find any grief, even though it's my own mother." Nelly's words were accompanied by a helpless raising of her shoulders.

Ika gave Nelly a quick hug. "You're off your guard and your mind is spinning, mine as much as yours. We thought we had time to think about the death, but now we have to arrange the funeral in a hurry. That's what it is, Nelly. And you have to get used to the idea that Mother doesn't need your attention anymore."

"I still feel she's calling me," Nelly acknowledged softly. "I can still see how sternly she looked across to the sliding doors as I came in, always late. It was never good enough. However often I came, however much I brought, it was always too little. However long I stayed, it was always too short. When I went away, I would stick out my tongue as I shut the kitchen door. It was childish but that's what I did. Let's go downstairs where it's warm, and we can begin to write out the envelopes."

It was indeed cold upstairs. Ika was stiff when she stood up. Nelly broke out again into a hoarse laugh as she struggled over the threshold and bumped into Ika on the dark landing.

"Do you remember how I used to carry you on my back down the stairs?" Ika whispered.

Nelly nodded. "You wouldn't be able to hold me now. I'm a good forty pounds heavier than you."

Moments later an atmosphere of quiet companionship spread throughout the house, a kind of bond, while they looked through the addresses Mother had written down.

Mother was to be buried on Tuesday. After the burial there would be a brief commemoration service and a reception in the church hall for the mourners. Coffee or tea, and a roll. Something simple.

"She'll be buried next to Father, won't she?" Ika asked Willem.

He nodded. "Yes, it's a double plot they bought together for that purpose. Her name and dates can be added to the headstone now."

The whole idea seemed abhorrent to Ika.

## CHAPTER NINETEEN

LATER THAT NIGHT the winter garden was finished.

"Do you want to stay here alone?" Willem had asked.

Of this Ika was sure. "Yes, you go on," she urged. "You've had to be without each other so much while Mother . . ."

Willem nodded, and Nelly just looked askance.

Once the noise of their footsteps had died away, it grew very quiet. Ika got right to work, coloring in the surfaces with soft pastel tints, drawing the stones on the path, all while struggling with the mechanism for the doors. Simone may be able to find a solution. Perhaps the sections of the wall could be placed on different rails so they could be pushed in front of one another. Otherwise there would need to be some type of folding system. She could see the plants in front of her eyes as if she were walking through her drawing.

Every so often Ika stood up and looked at Mother through the crack between the sliding doors. The front room had become a sort of sanctuary where she couldn't enter. The winter garden was around the front room, and she was the guard at the gate. She didn't find it so dreadful to look at Mother.

From the path of yellow pebbles, Ika walked along by the water section, where the stepping stones still had to be put into position. But not too far from one another; a child should be able to get across the water with ease. Abe, for example. She measured out a small step, stood up, and looked again at Mother. The face appeared even more still, more beautiful and soft. She seemed to be sinking away into herself, finally entering the rest of a winter garden. Mother's own winter garden.

Ika then realized that everything connected with Mother could be found in her own winter garden. Somehow the pastel shades had offset the strong smell of illness that emanated from the front room.

When it became light, she'd open the top window. But dawn was still hours away. Ika didn't think it unpleasant keeping watch over her, for it had been a long time since she'd been so close to Mother. "I'm here, Mother," she would whisper each time she looked up toward the front room.

Nelly did the preparation, which was certainly her right. It wasn't in any way horrific, but a caring task that had to be carried out—something Nelly was good at. Ika could see how carefully she did the work. And how caringly.

Mother had just been made ready when the bell rang. Ika saw

the black hearse through the window. She understood what it was. The coffin had arrived.

Ika wouldn't soon forget the shocked face of Abe, who had come along just as the coffin was about to be carried into the house.

The soberly dressed men filled the hallway with their discussion. The door into the room was a problem. The coffin would go in all right by tilting it, but how would they get it out on Tuesday morning?

Abe's eyes grew big. For his sake, Ika wished the men would quickly finish and then be on their way. Again they did a trial run, walking through into the back room and out its other door into the hall. This time was somewhat easier, yet still tight.

"Would it not be better to go out through the back door?" Ika asked.

The men froze in shocked silence.

"Brides and the dead go out through the *front* door," one of them said.

"But if that's not possible . . . ?"

"It'll have to work. Using the back door just isn't done."

"It would be better to go through the back door decently than to go out the front in a fuss," said Ika.

"I suppose you come from the city. They don't bother about this sort of thing any longer there." It sounded as if he had worked with city people.

"Auntie Ika, is Granny tied up in that coffin? Couldn't we just set her straight again once she's got through the door?" Abe whispered.

Ika took Abe to the kitchen. The men would have to figure out the problem with the coffin and the doors with Willem, who was now coming around the back.

Abe looked worried. "I think it's so nasty to have to go in a coffin like that. The Egyptians were embalmed, you know. Can they still do that?"

Ika smiled and stroked his spiky hair. "But things were much worse then. They used lye to embalm the dead. That's a kind of soda. But first they had to take out all their insides."

Both surprised and incredulous, Abe just shook his head. No, that was no way to do it. "I really wanted to go and play football, but I don't suppose I'd be allowed to do that now."

Ika saw through his attempt to take flight and nodded. "Don't worry. Off you go. I'll tell your mother."

Abe was already standing by the door. He turned around once more and asked, "How do you know all that stuff about the lye?"

She looked at him. *How much a child had to learn before he could be fitted for life*, she thought.

With Mother in the coffin now, she seemed much more distant, more of a dead person, less a mother. The peace with which Ika had been able to look at her the night before had all gone. Now she found it all but impossible to face the days ahead. And Tuesday was still to come.

Ika looked for a chance to talk to Nelly, who had found her

diversion in polishing and scrubbing. The window at the back had to be cleaned, the sink scoured, and the kitchen mopped. *What was the use?* Ika said to herself. *Who would notice it?* She couldn't follow Nelly around. The day seemed to have lost its pattern of time. Finally, around four o'clock, Nelly took a break for some coffee.

"I'm going home right away," Ika said. "Tomorrow I'll come back again."

Nelly looked at her absently, then down at her reddened hands. "If you want to. Everything's ready here. Anyway, you kept watch all last night. Tonight Willem will do it."

When Ika unlocked the door of her flat, she realized it had only been a week since she'd made the decision to go and see her mother. Only one week!

The flat was cold and dark. Ika switched on all the table lamps and closed the curtains. Then she took a long shower. She needed urgently to wash away the smell of illness. After her shower, she sank down on the sofa to look through her mail.

But the feeling of being at home didn't return to her, as if her home was back at her mother's again.

Twice she began to dial Simone's number, but stopped halfway through and hung up. She wanted to speak to Simone, yet didn't feel up to having to tell her that Mother was dead. Now Ika felt a bit more of her ordinary world, which she couldn't yet face. She sat on the threshold between the two worlds, between the two homes. While Simone had fitted wonderfully into the front room, there Simone had been an outsider. Here she'd be herself—Simone, the insider.

Just as Ika was making up her mind to go to bed with a hot-water bottle, the phone rang. So jolted was she by the unexpected sound, that she almost dropped the rubber bag. Knowing it would be Simone, she picked up the receiver.

"Oh, it's you," Simone said, as soon as Ika had said her name.

"What do you mean? Did you expect somebody else?"

"If you hadn't answered, I was planning to call the police next."

"Sorry, I don't follow you."

"Look out your window. I'm standing in the square in front of your flat."

Ika went as far as the telephone cord would allow her to in the direction of the window. Reaching and pulling back the curtain, she peered into the darkness and saw Simone squeezed into the telephone booth on the corner of the square. Her car was parked nearby with the lights still on. "Come up," Ika said. "What are you doing out so late?"

Simone had to sit down as soon as she entered Ika's flat, for she was extremely out of breath from climbing the stairs.

"We do have an elevator here, you know."

"I'm not that old yet," Simone puffed.

"But you *are* that overweight," Ika shot back.

Simone gave her a withering look. "So why did you come home?"

"I had to get away from there. I'm going back tomorrow though." She steered clear of the difficult question.

Simone nodded and said, "I saw the light on as I was driving past, so I thought I better call. You never know."

"What were you doing around here?"

"Pour me something to drink and then I'll tell you my troubles."

"Don't tell me it's something really bad."

Simone leaned back on the sofa. "Everything will be okay, but I was pretty angry this morning."

Ika searched the kitchen for something Simone might like, but with her not being home there wasn't much choice. A half bottle of vermouth was all she could find. So Ika filled a glass and set it down in front of Simone, then sat down in the chair opposite her. "Now tell me."

"Some formidable competition has raised its head. Two contracts were cancelled during the week, and this morning there was a fax from the Promenade Hotel that said they wanted us to complete the design of the winter garden, but *not* be involved in its maintenance. They've found a cheaper quote for that."

"I don't believe it! And who is this cheaper quote? Do you know the firm?"

"Never heard of it. A horticulturist's business. The Morning Star or something. Does that mean anything to you?"

"No. Is it a local firm?"

"I wouldn't know," said Simone. "But I'll find out and then pay them a visit. The scoundrels!"

The aggression in her voice did Simone good. She perked up visibly, though the vermouth pleased her less. "Filthy stuff, like old rubbish." But Simone went ahead and poured another glass, leaned back again, and said bleakly, "Maintenance was already on the low side. If I don't get more work, I'll have to fire someone. Winter's always a slack time for business. My hope is that your design will bring something in. A lot of business people go there. You never know how the ball rolls."

Ika didn't say much. She looked at Simone from under the table lamp. She wished she had a slice of cake or some kind of snack for her, something Simone would think was good and tasty. "Shall we order a pizza?" she asked suddenly and burst out laughing when she saw Simone's eager reaction.

"With olives and anchovies and lots of cheese. Make it two pizzas."

It gave them a strange feeling of unity to be eating out of a cardboard box together. It was delicious, too, though Simone ate far and away the greater amount.

Only when Simone was leaving did Ika finally tell her. "Tuesday is the funeral. You'll find the card tomorrow in your mailbox."

Simone looked as if she'd taken a blow to the head. It was rare to see her so speechless. Ika nearly had to laugh. It didn't suit Simone at all.

When Simone had left—still with a disconcerted look in her brown eyes—Ika turned her attention to her clothes. She ought to find something dark to wear to her mother's funeral.

Suddenly Ika thought of Mother's clothes, of her closet, and the pile of underwear that had fallen out just as she had died. They'd have to empty the closet now. She and Nelly. In fact, the whole house would have to be gone through and emptied. Ika broke out in a sweat at the very thought.

The house would have to be sold. It wouldn't be there anymore as Mother's house. The garden, as well, and the little path with the mosses. Other people would live and sleep there. Perhaps they would find it old-fashioned with its granite sink and brass tap. They might want to knock it down and rebuild.

Why did the thought hurt her so much? Ika had never really liked the house. For her it held nothing but painful memories. It was a dreadful house, with a hall full of water and anxiety and false light.

But imagine if it wasn't Mother's house anymore.

With a bang she shut the wardrobe door. It would have to be the dark blue raincoat, even if it was getting a bit threadbare.

Ika tried to sleep, but it turned into a night full of waking and dreaming. There was a single thought that had remained just below the surface. Why had she not gone right away to see Mr. Molenaar?

Did she not want to know about her past after all?

Between her waking moments she dreamed strange dreams, mixing up all the confused fragments of the past days. The throbbing of the airplanes, Dr. Spaan's cursing, Nelly and the coral necklace, the tilted coffin, Abe with a soup pan of lye, and Simone in a duel over a pizza.

Saturday morning began with a fine drizzle. While Ika was arranging things and looking after her plants, Simone's words came back to her. Ika was curious about the person who was frustrating their business plans so she looked in the professional horticulturists' guide for a firm called The Morning Star. It wasn't there, but the guide was over a year old. Perhaps the business had just started up.

She stood for a long time, staring at her design for the winter garden. It would be a pity if they couldn't look after the maintenance of the garden. One never knew what the garden would turn out to be after a few years. It would be quite a coincidence if another firm had the same combinations in mind as Ika.

Again she looked at the list of her plants: *Epimedium,* a late bloomer that stays green in the winter; *Helleboris foetidus,* stinking hellebore, which, in fact, doesn't stink and blooms as early as January; and *Hacouetia epipactus,* a spring bloomer with apple green flowers. They were not the easiest of plants, but they accentuated the atmosphere the winter garden must have. Peace and freshness, breathtaking in various shades of green and leaf formations, and a richness that had to be discovered, which literally drove one to the knees.

Ika hoped that The Morning Star understood this.

When Ika went in through the back door at four o'clock, Nelly was in the kitchen frying meat. It gave Ika such a homey feeling that she didn't want to go any further than the kitchen. She threw her coat over one chair and sat down on another.

She told Nelly that it felt as though Mother were still alive and in the front room peeling pears. Nelly had to laugh, for Mother never peeled pears in that room. She did that with her apron on and only in the kitchen. And she was right.

Nelly pointed to the stacks of dirty cups. "It's been busy here this afternoon. The minister stopped by along with a few elders and neighbors, and also the committee for the Women's Club, even though Mother never attended. We'll eat here. It'll be nicer for you."

There was something reverential about the atmosphere in the house. The fact that Mother lay behind the sliding doors wasn't in any way frightening. Yet it was still a reality they had to keep in mind.

Nelly cooked the endive just as Mother had always done, and it seemed peculiar to Ika that she enjoyed eating it so much. Previously she had never liked endive, nor had she ever cooked any for herself.

Ika looked over at Abe, who opened his mouth before his full fork like a young sparrow. Simone also ate this way, with such commitment. Ika burst out laughing when she thought about the pizza.

"Do they really bring it right to your house?" Abe asked.

"Yep," Ika replied. "You just make a phone call and, before you know it, somebody comes along on a motor scooter with a little insulated box on the back to keep the pizza hot."

Dirk-Willem listened with his mouth wide open. "On a motor scooter?" he asked just to make sure.

Ika nodded, noticing how he sat playing with his food.

Dirk-Willem dropped his fork for the second time. "I want to be a pizza man when I grow up, one on a motor scooter," he said, thoroughly convinced.

"Well, for the time being, you stick to finishing that endive," was the sharp comment Nelly made regarding Dirk-Willem's plans for his future.

"Phew!" the pizza man protested, and then endive flew into Willem's hair.

## CHAPTER TWENTY

THE FUNERAL WAS LESS of an ordeal than Ika had feared. There were certainly some curious looks, yet she felt unaffected by them. Those gathered there didn't approach her to express their condolences personally. Anyhow, it wasn't very crowded. Mother didn't have much family. Nor had she many acquaintances.

The old cemetery, which Ika remembered as a windy garden with straight gravel paths, had pleased her greatly. They had built a new chapel and cleaned many of the old graves, so that the grounds had taken on a whole new look. Beautiful bushes and varied plantings covered the place now, all situated on different planes. It looked like the newer graves were resting on the slope of low hills. Basically a bowl-shaped hollow, the cemetery showed itself as if protected by the rising greenery that surrounded it.

The place had taken Ika by surprise, and she was instantly curious as to who maintained it. It looked to be more than the work of the local council gardens department. That much was clear. A landscape architect who knew about gardens had obviously been employed here.

The voice of the young minister wasn't saying much of anything new but mostly gave a smattering of clichés. Ika knew before he had finished one sentence what the next would be. " 'All flesh is as grass, which blooms today, but when the wind passes over it . . . and the place thereof shall know it no more.' " He then did his best to say something personal about Mother, but he didn't know a whole lot. Mother didn't let herself be known.

The birds did a better job of it. There were doves in the trees. Turtledoves that called to one another and to the people below. Ika found it easy to listen to the doves, to shut out the minister completely.

Nelly cried from time to time, her eyes becoming redder with each outburst of emotion. Because she had no lipstick on that day, she looked extra pale.

Willem tugged periodically at his tight black suit, which was really his wedding suit.

Leaning against Nelly was Dirk-Willem, who stood like a flushed little angel with his thumb in his mouth.

Ika smiled when she looked at Abe. He was counting the turtle-doves. She could see it from his eyes and his murmuring lips.

Why couldn't they attend the funeral by themselves, just she and Nelly and Willem and the boys? Why all this pomp, with the mourning cars and people in their black hats, who, in their funeral clothes, smelled of mothballs?

Aunt Klaar in particular stank for an hour in the open air. Apart from her, there were a few distant nephews and nieces, the neighbor, and some elders from the church. All of them were people who came to do the decent and respectable thing, mostly because they had received a mourning card. People with appropriate expressions on their faces, but who added nothing.

Ika was glad, however, that Simone had come. She stood a little to the back with her hands in the pockets of her coat, bareheaded and serious, as if prepared to intervene in the event that anything went wrong. Ika tried to imagine such a scenario.

With dismay, Ika noticed that the minister had finished. He was soon followed by the drawling voice of Jan Jonker, who talked about drinking coffee and thanking all those involved. Had it all passed over her head?

It seemed Ika had used up all her emotions. Even when the coffin was lowered into the ground, her eyes remained dry.

Her heart told her that it was good here, a beautiful garden. There was something very peaceful about the cooing of the doves, making Ika feel that Mother was truly at rest now, at home.

She would come back here again. Tomorrow afternoon, when all the people had left. Then she could walk alone along the gravel path. Only then could she say good-bye to Mother. Not now, not at this moment, not while all these people were here.

The procession began to move away from the grave. From the church hall wafted the smell of coffee, greeting everyone. At this the blackened crowd revived and found their tongues again. Ika walked with Simone to her car and silently watched as Simone got in and drove off.

Rubbing her arm, Ika retraced her steps back to the graveside. She couldn't leave Nelly standing there alone. Ika sensed Simone's sympathy as she walked.

❦

When they had arrived home, Nelly wasted no time in translating her emotions into deeds. She dove right in, beginning with clearing out the closet. On the bed where Mother had been lying, two piles were growing ever higher. Everything, down to the still unused damask napkins, was being counted.

Ika couldn't watch so she went to find Abe who was in the garden. He was angrily digging out the *Doronicum*. "Why are you doing that?" Ika asked.

"*She* said I had to," he grumbled between his teeth and plunged the spade deep into the ground. With his head, he had made a movement toward the house, where Nelly was.

"Now?" Ika couldn't understand Nelly's hurry, but was touched she didn't want to leave the plant behind. Ika took the spade from Abe and stuck it under the root ball, while Abe fetched an orange crate from the shed. Carefully she let the plant slide off the spade. "Have you a place for it in your garden?"

"Do you want it?" Abe asked, his eyes lighting up as if pleased to make her happy.

"I . . . I don't think it would grow very well on my balcony," she said hesitantly.

Abe shook his head, then filled the hole with loose earth. "And your friend, the fat one, does she have a garden?"

Ika looked at him a bit surprised. What was it now between her and Abe? Was it a kind of love at first sight, or just the blood relationship? "Abe, I want to go back to the grave," she said bluntly. "Would you like to come along?"

Abe threw down the spade and wiped his hands on his pants. "Can I?"

Together they walked the gravel path that led to the cemetery. It seemed colder than it had been a few hours earlier and the wind had picked up. A few last leaves rolled and rustled across the grass.

The grave was already closed over, the mound of earth beside it now gone. The planks at the graveside had also disappeared, and a layer of sand had been spread among the green of the grass. Still, nothing betrayed what lay beneath.

Abe laid a withered red leaf of ivy on the grave, pressing the sand around its stem to make sure it didn't blow away.

It was good to be here with Abe, to smooth down the sand and to listen to the trees.

As Ika continued to stand at Mother's grave, Abe got restless and appeared to begin exploring the cemetery. Ika wondered if perhaps she was opening up within herself, a great open space, with slopes like here. No obstacles. Nothing to drag her down. No place for bad thoughts.

Voices and the crunch of wheels on the gravel brought Ika back to reality. Besides Abe's voice, she heard the voice of an older man. When she saw a wheelchair coming around the corner she knew she wasn't mistaken. It was Mr. Molenaar. He looked fragile, with his legs under a lap robe.

Abe's cheerful voice reverberated through the cemetery. "This is Mr. Molenaar. I told him you were here. He remembers you from the past."

A strange tremble crossed Ika's mouth as if after all that she'd been through, she was only now going to have to cry dreadfully. But all that came out was the sound of a single moan, which left a sharp painful trace in her throat.

She gripped Mr. Molenaar's cold soft hand, seeing that he had more difficulty with tears than did she.

Abe's voice rattled on—about the funeral and about the doves.

The teacher rolled his wheelchair to the sandy patch, vacant except for the ivy leaf. Abe was now quiet, no more stories to tell.

When Mr. Molenaar had stared at the ground long enough, he turned his thin wrinkled cheek toward Ika. "I knew you would be here, Ikabod."

"Mother wrote about you," she said. "I haven't had time yet . . ." His perceptive watching reminded Ika of years before. He had looked like this in class too. She lowered her eyes.

Mr. Molenaar tapped her hand. "Come see me if you can find the time. I'm nearly always in my room."

Ika heard the crunch of those wheels in her head for a long time afterward. And later when she was at home with Nelly, making arrangements with Mother's house and things, again and again the wheels of Mr. Molenaar's wheelchair crunched their way through everything.

The feeling had two sides to it. Ika was pleased she had met him, yet was afraid of the consequences. She wondered if she could visit him and express that she didn't want to know anything. Not to talk about the past. Not to lose the space within her. Not to keep on seeing images from the past. That tearing-of-cellophane feeling must not come back again.

"If you can find the time," he'd said. But did he not mean, "If you can find the *courage*"?

Simone had been busy. Despite her gloomy predictions earlier, she knew of enough new projects for which she had a fair chance to compete. For now that the competition had grown more fierce, it became more than ever a question of how to price her calculations more keenly, to ensure more work came their way in the future.

Meanwhile Ika met with the manager of the Promenade Hotel to discuss the design of the winter garden. Unfortunately, he knew very little about gardens. It was only when Ika mentioned the estimate that she felt she had his full attention. He suddenly sat up straight in his chair and sputtered, "That's too expensive!"

"But we planned it according to your budget," Ika protested.

The man sank back again, then lightly tapped his fingertips against one another, perhaps to signal he had the matter well under control. "There is, I think, some competition arising in your line of business," he said knowingly.

Ika bit back the sharp comment she was tempted to blurt out. *This is no way to do business, to quibble about the budget afterward,* she thought. "The design cannot be separated from its realization. That was our condition for taking on the project," she said, hoping to forestall him.

The man nodded. "Yes, yes. I certainly heard as much from your superior."

❧

When Ika left the office with the commission for laying out the garden literally in her pocket, she stifled back a huge sigh of relief as she stepped into the elevator. It was just as well that her superior was still sitting behind her own chaotic desk, for she undoubtedly would've been driven over the edge by the meeting Ika had just attended.

The negotiations had concluded with hotel management giving the nod for Berger's Landscape Gardening to forge ahead with the project. If Simone wanted to get Chinese takeout now, Ika wouldn't say no. Simone had laughed at the suggestion, then immediately made the call to order the food.

While they ate, they talked seriously about The Morning Star. This problem couldn't be pushed away any longer; it had become a pressing issue, requiring swift action on their part. So they decided that Simone should go and meet with the owner. It would only harm things to continue to avoid each other. Better to have a friendly conversation and come to some kind of arrangement.

"He seems reasonable," said Simone after she'd called for an appointment—high praise for a competitor.

Ika didn't want to leave the office before Simone would return, so she took some time to finish off Mother's personal and financial affairs. Willem had asked her to do this. He wasn't very good at such things and there was much to do. Dealing with the real estate agent, gas and electricity bills, and home and health insurance companies. Always the same story, although Ika got used to responsibilities.

Working on Mother's affairs brought to mind her promise to Mr. Molenaar. Why did she keep avoiding making an appointment? The past few nights she had promised herself to phone him the following day. It seemed more logical to visit him at night, yet in the gray light of November she still held back from making the call, the funeral being too fresh in her mind.

First, there must come an end to the things that were threatening. The memory she now had of Mother had to endure. Perhaps the space within her couldn't yet be filled. For the same reason, she couldn't see Nelly, either, even though she was welcome. But she did want to see Abe.

It was confusing. Years without any contact and then all at once so involved with each other at Mother's death. Could it be that Mother's passing away first had to find its place, to become a part of her? Twice during the afternoon she had to call Nelly for information. Both times her heart was in her throat. Just to call and make contact, to say something, to ask something. Ika wasn't used to this.

It was already dark when Ika heard Simone's heavy steps in the corridor. She looked at her watch and pushed Mother's papers to one side. Her eyes were fastened on the door so as not to miss Simone's expression when she came in.

The door swung open, and Ika couldn't help but laugh. Simone was attempting to hide behind two armfuls of greenery. "I don't need to ask," Ika said, taking the biggest Kentia palm from Simone. "I see he has literally *palmed* you off!"

"I'd like to have seen you do any better. Kentias, young lady, and a bonsai section to die for." Simone gave her chair a push to slide it over to Ika's desk.

Ika was glad she had just made fresh coffee. She filled two mugs and then removed the package of fresh macaroons—which Simone had just bought at the baker's—from her bag. "These look delicious," Ika said. "Now tell all!"

Simone slurped her coffee cheerfully and began, "He may be an egotistical nurseryman, but at least he's genuine. He's just started up a section for orange plants, some new varieties but with the old-fashioned ones too. Right now he has oleanders and camellias in bloom. He rents out a few of his greenhouses in the winter to private individuals for plants in tubs, like fuchsias and bay trees. It's a clever business. He has very little work to do on it. Only make sure that it's frost-free. Because he has so little work in the winter, he's begun designing gardens, beginning with a couple of jobs locally. And both clients were quite satisfied with his work.

"Well, that may be so, but then he doesn't have to score off us." Ika protested against what seemed to be too charitable a tale. "Let him stay on his own turf."

Simone shook her head. "But that's just it. He has gladioli here in the neighborhood. I've even seen some of his designs myself. The

Morning Star is in the village where your mother lived. The cemetery grounds are his work."

Ika had the feeling that his name was on the tip of her tongue. She knew it, yet couldn't recall it no matter how hard she tried. She opened her mouth but then clamped it shut again when Simone pulled the card from her cluttered handbag. After smoothing it flat on the side of her skirt, Simone stuck it out over the desk to Ika. Ika turned it over. " 'The Morning Star. Garden Center and Landscape Gardeners. Bart Hogerveer, Canal Road.' "

Simone asked if she was hungry, for Ika had gone all white. "Are you going to faint?"

Ika passed the card back. After taking a deep breath, she said, "I know him."

"What?"

"I know Bart Hogerveer. I know him from way back. He was a boyfriend."

"A boyfriend?" Simone was almost shouting now and she had a puzzled look on her face. "From the past? I had it in my mind that you never had a boyfriend . . ." She stopped without finishing the sentence, yet her mouth remained open.

Half smiling, Ika made a gesture of excuse. "Just this one. We were very young. Bart Hogerveer's father used to have a nursery for perennial plants on Heren Street, the main street of the village."

"Well, that just takes the biscuit!" Simone said.

"Then that will make two you have eaten."

❦

Later, when they had put on their coats and were standing ready to leave, Ika suddenly told Simone about the decision that had been nestling in the space in her life without being noticed. "Simone, I have to do something about it now. I mean, if I stay afraid of the troubles of the past, then I'll always stay the same. I must draw a line under it. At some point I must take responsibility for my own life. There's nobody to blame anymore. I won't be here tomorrow. I've got to go and speak to someone about my past."

Simone switched off the light, closed the door and, in the semi-darkness of the corridor, said, "I don't understand you one bit, Ika. But as far as I know, the man's not married and he despises women."

"Mr. Molenaar? He never married, but to despise women. . .?"

"Are we talking about the same person?" asked Simone. "His name is Hogerveer."

## CHAPTER TWENTY-ONE

THE ROOM WAS JUST LIKE the teacher himself, warm and restful looking. Ika stood in front of the window and looked out. There were people working in the garden. A large basket of bulbs sat in the middle of the path. On the backs of the men's blue coveralls was emblazoned *The Morning Star*.

Mr. Molenaar was preparing coffee in his tiny kitchen. He still walked around inside a little but was making hard work of it. He moved more with his hands than with his legs. Again and again he would grab the back of a chair, the edge of the kitchen counter, or the doorjamb and hold on tight to heave himself further along.

Ika remembered from earlier days that when Mr. Molenaar stood in front of the class, if he was standing for a long time, he would use his hands to lean on a chair or desk. His knees had given up on him.

"They're putting in bulbs," Ika said in answer to his question about what she was looking at.

"Wonderful," he replied contentedly. "That's a promise of spring."

Ika carried the coffee to the small table by the window. They sat at opposite sides. Now that she was here, she could hardly believe she'd doubted whether or not to come. Nothing seemed more logical than to be sitting here.

"I had trouble with my car this morning," she told him. "It wouldn't start. Quite often it does that in the winter. Fortunately I was able to borrow a car from the business. It's that white one over there," she said, pointing.

Mr. Molenaar was still able to read what was written on the car's door without needing his glasses. *Berger's Landscape Gardening.* "Do you enjoy your job?" he asked.

She nodded as she warmed her hands on the coffee cup. "Very much. I'm allowed to design gardens, and it's been rewarding to make such beautiful things. My most recent project, which I worked on when I was at Mother's, involved a winter garden. I think it turned out lovely."

"A winter garden?" repeated Mr. Molenaar. "Yes. That really is something. I'm sure that's a project you could work on at your mother's." He pushed the empty cup away. Then his eyes turned serious, and his hand shook a little as he took his hankie out of his pocket to wipe the sides of his mouth.

Ika recognized this action too. With a smile, she nodded.

"I came to the village shortly after the war," he began. "The village was smaller then. People knew a lot about each other and they also knew how to talk about each other. I went into lodgings at Mrs. Donker's, the widow. You knew her well. On the avenue, remember? She had a daughter, Machteld, who had a soft and sweet nature. I lost my heart to her.

"Machteld had a friend named Nelly Boerema. Yes, your mother. She was a few years younger than Machteld, but they had been friends for years. Machteld often went over to Nelly's house, in the manse. Sometimes I went along too. I found it very interesting talking to your grandfather. He was an exceptional man, stately and strict. But then, you know that already, don't you? I always had the feeling he knew better than God himself, but I didn't dare to say that out loud at the time.

"And I didn't dare ask Machteld to go out with me, partly from embarrassment and partly because of the practical implications. I would've had to find other lodgings. At that time, it wasn't done to sleep under the same roof as your girlfriend.

"I wish I hadn't waited so long, because eventually another man came for her. Dirk de Haan. Yes, child, your father. They started going out with each other, and I had to look on. That was hard.

"But things didn't turn out very well for Machteld. She began to look more and more delicate. It was tuberculosis, but it was discovered far too late. She was admitted to a sanatorium.

"Dirk went to the sanatorium regularly, at least in the beginning. Nelly sometimes went with him. She was overwhelmed with sadness. She kept coming to see Machteld's mother, and we got on well with each other. It did us all good to talk about Machteld.

"Then suddenly it was all over. Just before Machteld's death it was all over. Nelly didn't come anymore. Not even when Machteld died. Not even for the funeral.

"Stories started to go around about Nelly. She was supposed to be pregnant, but nobody knew by whom. For a whole year she never left the manse. People never knew whether it was a girl or a boy."

"It was a girl," Ika said.

The teacher had to bring his handkerchief into service again, this time to wipe his eyes. "When you were baptized, the whole village was turned upside down. I'll never forget that service." A shudder passed across the teacher's narrow shoulders. He looked at her, and the whites of his eyes had become red. "The name you were given, Ikabod. Oh, child, you should have seen the way your grandfather looked at you and your mother. From that moment onwards, I never darkened the door of the church. It had nothing to do with the Heavenly Father. You were called Ikabod, and you cried like a young lamb bleating.

"Of course, people were making guesses about who the father might be. Dirk's name was mentioned, and mine was too. I didn't dare go near your mother. Leaving the church had created problems for me at school. And spending time with her would've put people on the wrong track. 'The teacher at the manse. I told you so.' Our friendship would have been a confession. And I had no confession to make."

It was quiet again. Restlessly the teacher's hand stroked the tablecloth.

An icy cold lump had grown in the place where Ika's heart had been. Swallowing didn't help. When she fidgeted in her seat, it shocked him back to the present.

"After some time, when you were already a year old, Dirk did after all marry your mother. Finally your grandfather had found a compromise. If Dirk agreed to marry Nelly, he would be absolved of any guilt. It would be made clear from the pulpit that there was no blame attached to him. It must've been one of your grandfather's best sermons—the poor disappointed man who had lost his first love, and who now sacrificed himself for a fallen woman and her child."

It was an unbearable feeling that the man who had made Ika's life so impossible was her father all along. She'd had no mother, and the dream that somewhere there was a man who could be her father, even this dream would have to be given up now. This was worse than all the other options. She had been able to bring herself to consider all the possibilities—if Mother had been raped, or let down, or even if she'd gotten herself mixed up with many others. But why had Mother never told her exactly what happened? Why had she always kept the photo of Machteld on display? Who was tormenting whom by this? Was it to keep the feeling of guilt alive?

Why did people plague one another with reproach over and

over again? It seems someone was always hounding someone else, but why? Had her mother and father nevertheless done their best to make it work? Did it not work?

And Nelly? How had they come together for Nelly? Had the bitterness grown so much that in the course of time it became more and more clear they had made a big mistake? Why would people allow themselves to live out their lives as a great indictment? Or should she see this whole thing as the consequence of the inability to do good, the inclination to do evil?

This would certainly have been Grandfather's opinion. But how could he not have seen that with his planning he was keeping God and His promises out of it? How he collaborated with great evil!

Thoughts fluttered back and forth through Ika's head. How long had she been sitting here? Time seemed to have stood still.

"Why did he do it?" asked Ika. "Why did he let my grandfather bully him like that?"

"I don't know," Mr. Molenaar answered. "A feeling of guilt about Machteld, or maybe because of the influence of your grandfather's power. A year later Dirk was on the church council. Perhaps he wanted to do a good deed in the eyes of the village."

"But would you marry someone for reasons like that, if you couldn't get along with them?"

"Maybe that wasn't the case at the time, child. Maybe they both hoped that happiness would follow."

"It was me then. I was the misfortune at home they kept coming up against. It was I who ruined their lives. That's why Nelly had to make good what was wrong with me. And that's why they loved Nelly. Why did God allow it? Why did Father not legitimize me later? Why did he go on hassling Mother as he did, as if she alone was guilty of what happened with me? Surely he knew the truth. Why did Mother start to think it was my fault? She was in the know as well."

The teacher pushed his hand over the tablecloth to Ika's hands, which were grimly clutching at the edge of the table. His hands were even colder than hers.

"Child, people always look for guilt outside themselves. A person chooses the role of the victim. You reminded them of their sin, and so you became the scapegoat, and your grandfather went along with that."

"Oh, I can't live with this!" Ika jumped up from her chair. She had to get away.

But the look in the teacher's eyes caused her to sit down again. Ika was surprised, for he was laughing now. He was laughing, yet there were tears streaming down his thin cheeks.

"Listen, child. Do listen. You came back. You who were guiltless of all this came back to take care of her. In spite of everything. God must indeed love you, to have allowed you to do that. Who do you think you were like in doing that? Now tell me."

Ika closed her eyes and the image of the winter garden overwhelmed her. Behind her eyelids the words of Isaiah drifted past and all at once miraculously fell into place among the greenery, the moss, the water, and the path with the little yellow pebbles. "Behold, I will do a new thing; now it shall spring forth . . . I will make a way in the wilderness, and rivers in the desert. Fear not, for I have redeemed thee, I have called thee by thy name; thou art mine."

The ice-cold lump in her chest freed itself from the dark area of pain, and the first drops of water searched for a way to become the beginning of a stream over which the sun would create a rainbow.

And Mr. Molenaar saw it. He stumbled up from his chair and went to fetch his Bible. The verses from Isaiah grew wet with tears.

The teacher stood waving at the window. Ika looked one more time at the shrunken figure behind the flowerpots. She composed herself and then waved back.

She couldn't stay any longer. She still had to visit Mother's grave, then see Nelly, and maybe toward evening make it over to Simone's. She had to see people now, and they had to see her. They would see something new in her, even if she told them nothing.

The sun cast its stripes through the low clouds. With nobody in the parking lot or walking around, the cemetery was very quiet. Ika made her way down the gravel path toward the grave.

Abe's leaf was still in the ground, there on Mother's grave, and the doves were still in the trees. There was much to see. She pressed her hands against her glowing cheeks. God was there. Everywhere.

Beside Abe's leaf Ika made a handprint for Mother in the still loose sand. A hand was good. They had never really kissed much.

She then started back, as it was beginning to get dusky. The garden was growing wintery. Someone had just swept the place, and piles of fallen leaves still lay in a row near the fence. There were also empty baskets that had held bulbs before. Bart had been busy.

While Ika was fumbling in her handbag for the car keys, a vehicle drove into the parking lot. *The Morning Star, Garden Center and Landscape Gardeners* was written on its side.

She waited till the vehicle had stopped beside her. The driver was out in a flash and said with an amused expression on his face, "So Berger's Landscape Gardening is at it again. Sight-seeing today, are we?"

The wind blew through his blond hair. He became hesitant, and his eyes slowly narrowed.

Ika took a step forward and greeted him. "Hello, Bart!"

# Two Women, Two Different Eras, Two Terrific Novels

## Nothing in Her Life Had Prepared Her For This

Set against the backdrop of today's Israel, this is a story about the power of forgiveness, the cost of mercy, and the search for safe haven from the storms of life. Following Abigail MacLeod from her Midwest home to the Middle East, *Wings of Refuge* interweaves the lives of three women and their stories of suffering and redemption.

*Wings of Refuge* by Lynn Austin

## If the Truth Is Revealed, Will She Lose All She's Grown to Love?

An orphanage is the only home Sarah Matthews has ever known until she is whisked away to a wealthy widow's home. Why would this elderly woman, a stranger, want her company? Dorothea Blake has reasons she isn't revealing, but when a visitor unknowingly stumbles upon the truth, he puts Sarah at risk of losing everything she holds dear.

*The Maiden of Mayfair* by Lawana Blackwell

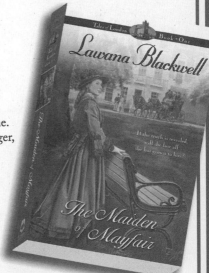

BETHANYHOUSE

11400 Hampshire Avenue S.
Minneapolis, MN 55438